Geronimo Stilton

THE KEEPERS OF THE EMPIRE

THE FOURTEENTH ADVENTURE IN THE KINGDOM OF FANTASY

Scholastic Inc.

Published by Scholastic Inc., *Publishers since 1920*, 557 Broadway, New York, NY 10012. SCHOLASTIC and associated logos are trademarks and/or registered trademarks of Scholastic Inc.

Stilton is the name of a famous English cheese. It is a registered trademark of the Stilton Cheese Makers' Association.

Library of Congress Cataloging-in-Publication Data available

ISBN 978-1-338-75692-0

Text by Geronimo Stilton
Original title *I custodi del Regno della Fantasia*
Cover by Silvia Bigolin
Art Director: Iacopo Bruno
Graphic Designer: Pietro Piscitelli / theWorldofDOT
Illustrations by Danilo Barozzi, Ivan Bigerella, Silvia Bigolin, Carla Debernardi, Danilo Loizedda, Alessandro Muscillo, and Christian Aliprandi
Graphics by Marta Lorini
Special thanks to Shannon Decker
Translated by Emily Clement
Interior design by Kay Petronio

10 9 8 7 6 5 4 3 2 1   21 22 23 24 25

Printed in China   62

First edition, November 2021

An Empire
to Save

Dear Rodent Friends,

I'm jumping out of my fur with excitement!

Together, we're about to explore a fantastic world that has been restored to its mousetastic glory after two thousand years . . .

the Empire of Fantasy!

Can you believe it? When Winglet, the daughter of the Queen of the Fairies, was crowned, this wondrous world was reborn. Now the young Rebel Empress reigns over an enormouse realm! After centuries of separation, the lands that once made up the empire have been magically reunified, and their harmony has been restored.

1

New people have come from far and wide, uniting with the Kingdom of Fantasy. Everyone here is much happier!

But a MENACING SHADOW looms over this era of discovery and growth . . .

Something dark threatens to endanger the peace and happiness of the whole empire.

This is a threat that only a band of true HEROES can stop. They must be brave, but also very, very creative!

They must put their differences aside and stand against what comes, together. Their DEEDS will be remembered forever in the Empire of Fantasy, and their story will inspire as only the best stories can.

That's a promise from your friend, *Geronimo Stilton*!

AN UPSIDE-DOWN ATTIC

Let's start in order, or should I say . . . disorder! That Sunday, Creepella von Cacklefur dragged me out of bed to begin a new project: organizing my **attic**!

I hadn't even needed my alarm clock, because at the crack of dawn she was standing outside my window, shouting, "Get up, my little cheese puff! Don't be a lazybones! The **sun** has been up for four minutes already! There's work to be done!"

Holey cheese, poor me!

I was very, very, verrrrry tired. The night before, I had stayed late at the office to finish a special article about tourism on Mouse Island and — oops, where are my manners? I haven't even introduced myself!

My name is Stilton, *Geronimo Stilton*, and

I run *The Rodent's Gazette*, the most famouse newspaper on Mouse Island.

As I was saying, I had gone to bed late and I was hoping to sleep in a bit, but once Creepella gets an idea in her **HEAD** . . . there's no stopping her!

"Coming, coming!" I sighed, scurrying out of bed and getting **DRESSED** in the twitch of a whisker.

As soon as I opened the door, Creepella walked into my house and said, "Quick, I've already prepared boxes for your things. We need to make room!"

Then she looked at me with narrowed eyes. "Tomorrow, my friend Vampiro Moviemouse is arriving in New Mouse City for a **HORROR** movie convention, and he needs a place to sleep. You

Coming, coming!

didn't forget, right? We're going to turn your attic into a dark, creaky bedroom full of spiders for him. Ah, it will feel just like home!"

Cheesy creampuffs! This was going to be a lot of work. After all, I'm a sentimental mouse. It had been years since I'd **cleaned** out my attic!

The moment we set paw in the attic, Creepella cried, "Bats and rats! How long has it been since you organized up here? This place is a mess!"

I mumbled, "Well, I've had a lot of work to do, and I'm always behind . . ."

Creepella was right! There were stacks — no, piles — no, **MOUNTAINS** of stuff everywhere!

"We'll have to start somewhere," Creepella said, sighing. "First, let's get rid of these books. You have so many of them!" She pointed a paw at a stack of heavy volumes.

My *Encyclopedia of Rat Linguistics* set of one-hundred-and-thirty-volumes? Just the thought of getting rid of it made my heart shatter into a thousand mousely pieces! That encyclopedia was a part of my personal history!

"Let's start somewhere else," I suggested, my whiskers wobbling.

Creepella sighed. "Okay, let's take care of these!" She picked up a stack of heavy binders.

Moldy mozzarella! "Oh no, that's my collection of cheese labels from around the world! I need them!" My poor paws were sweating. "Can't we get rid of something else?"

"What about that?" she said, pointing to a big bookshelf.

"But those are the cheese rinds that I still need to archive!" I squeaked.

Creepella frowned. "At this rate, we're not going to throw out anything! You need to make more space and get rid of all this junk!"

Cheese and crackers, she was right. I took a deep

breath and began to empty the **shelves**.

Puff! Pant!

When we were done, I was so tired I could barely lift

a paw. But we had managed to clean the place up!

Creepella smiled. "This is going to be spooktacular! In this corner, we can put a nice comfortable coffin for evenings full of nightmares, and over there we'll put a spacious wardrobe for guests. I'm proud of you!"

I was happy, too. I looked around the open, organized attic. Suddenly, I noticed that something was missing . . .

"Wait, what happened to my wooden *train set*?" I sputtered, my heart in my throat.

Creepella shrugged. "Oh, that old piece of junk? I threw it out!"

Crusty creampuffs! That was my favorite train! My first toy!

My aunt Sweetfur had given it to me when I was just a **mouselet,** and I really loved it. I had to get it back!

Quick as a cat, I raced down the stairs, but as soon as I set paw outside the front door . . .

The Rat Rubbish truck sped away!

Creepella walked up beside me. "What are you so worried about, my cheese puff?"

I tried to explain. "That was my **favorite** toy from when I was a mouselet. I have to get it back!"

Creepella slapped her forehead with one paw. "I'm so sorry! I should have asked you before I tossed it. I think they're taking it to the flea market. If you want, I can go with —"

Before she could finish, I had jumped into the car and was headed for the New Mouse City Flea Market!

The rodent in the **truck** had just finished

unloading at a merchant's booth, next to another mountain of objects.

How would I find my train in the middle of all that **STUFF**?!

But just then I spotted it, sticking out between a tennis racket and a lamp shaped like a wheel of cheese! I reached

out to grab the train
but lost my balance and
tripped on a spinning top.
I did a triple somersault and
ended up *falling* snoutdown on the
ground. I was out cold!

A FANTASTIC WORLD

When I woke up again, the toy train had disappeared — and so had the flea market! There were still other stalls all around me, but they were very, very strange!

One was overflowing with souvenirs: giant footprints, dragon scales, unicorn figurines . . .

Another displayed colorful little clouds that changed shape from second to second.

Yet another had shining armor in every size and color!

Holey cheese, this wasn't the New Mouse City Flea Market!

Where was I?

An aroma lingered in the air that was both sharp and sweet. Hmm . . . it was so familiar.

Just then someone shouted.

"Nuts! Nice fresh nuts! Who wants a roasted nut?"

What kind of nuts were these?

I looked around and saw that the shouts were coming from a small fellow who was as round as a snowman. He was roasting **nuts** over a fire. But these were no ordinary nuts. They were blue!

I had no idea what these were, but the smell coming from them was whisker-licking good!

A hooded figure rushed by the booth, riding on the back of a majestic **white tiger**. In a playful voice, she said to the merchant, "Give me two packets, please. One for me, and one for my friend!"

As soon as I recognized her, my heart danced with happiness: It was **Winglet**, the Rebel Empress! My heart leaped all over again when I saw her.

That's what the fragrance in the air was — the essence of the fairies! And that's where I had ended up: in the **kingdom of the fairies**, the heart of the Empire of Fantasy!

The vendor handed two packets to Winglet, turned back to his booth, and kept shouting.

Meanwhile, Winglet climbed down from her tiger and hugged me tightly.

"**Knight**, you're here!"

she cried. "I'm so happy to see you again."

"Winglet!" I said, a smile stretching all the way across my snout. "Now I recognize you, even

How splendid!

though you're hiding under that cloak!"

Winglet let out her familiar laugh. "Now and then I like to disguise myself, to take a break from the life of an empress! I want to be free to go wherever I like and meet some of the new people who have come to live here since the reunification of the empire. You'll see how many there are!" She grinned. "We discover more and more every day. The Empire of Fantasy is truly LIMITLESS and constantly changing! If only we could manage to — Oh, you must taste one of these!"

Winglet hadn't changed a bit. Even though she was a crowned empress, she hadn't lost the lively spirit of the Rebel Princess!

Though I couldn't help noticing that there seemed to be a glimmer of worry in her eyes . . . but maybe I was mistaken!

Winglet handed me one of the steaming packets and said, "This is a specialty of the Rolling

Kingdom, a new part of the empire. Down there, everything is round: the houses, the inhabitants, even the trees!"

I crunched on one of those cobalt-blue **NUTS**. Wow, it was whisker-licking good!

"Even Dawn wants one," said Winglet with a laugh.

The white tiger was eyeing my snack with a smile that showed off their **fangs**.

SQUEAK! HOW TERRIFYING!

Help yourself!

I held out a paw to offer Dawn one of the nuts, and it disappeared in the twitch of a whisker!

"Dawn appreciated it!" Winglet said, stroking the tiger's fur.

"M-my p-pleasure!" I spluttered, **_pale_** as a ball of mozzarella.

Winglet climbed up onto the white tiger's back and motioned for me to follow. "Come on, Knight. I want you to see how wonderful our new empire is! You're very lucky, because an important **EVENT** is coming up. These merchant stalls are just the beginning!"

I looked at Winglet and realized that she looked a lot like her mother, Blossom. She seemed a bit more confident than the last time I'd seen her. I could tell that the empress was calmer, a little more grown-up . . .

"**Hold on tight!**" she hollered, spurring Dawn on.

I could barely squeak before we took off like

a flash! We **wove** between two carts, dashed through a line of trees, jumped over a ditch, ran up a hill, pushed through a hedge, and squeezed under a fence. At last, we reached an enormouse arch with a SIGN above it. The sign read:

Welcome to the magnificent,
incomparable,
miraculous,
incredible,
astonishing . . .
Fantasy Fair!

THE FANTASY FAIR

I was ready to leap out of my fur with curiosity! Winglet proudly announced, "Each community has been given a spot at the fair to exhibit everything their KINGDOM has to offer!"

"How fabumouse," I breathed.

We passed under the arch and were met with a most mousetastic sight!

We were surrounded by color, sounds, and smells. The sky was filled with hot-air balloons, blimps, and extraordinary flying machines.

There were creatures I had never seen before, like tremendous giants that fluttered here and there on tiny fairy wings.

All around, I could see musicians, dancers, tightrope walkers, jugglers, mimes, puppeteers, flower sellers, painters, cooks, craftspeople, inventors, and sculptors. Everyone performed or brought exhibits to display.

Nearby, a woman with glowing golden skin had gathered rays of sunlight and played them like the strings of a **HARP**!

Three gnomes performed incredible acrobatics, jumping and tumbling on huge multicolored mushrooms!

I felt like a little mouselet again, when Grandfather William took me to the New Mouse City Amousement Park for the first time!

"How marvemouse!" I cried, my *heart* stretching with joy like string cheese. Then I turned and realized that Winglet had disappeared.

Squeak! I had been so distracted by the fair that I hadn't noticed!

Suddenly, a voice cried out from above. "Watch out, Knight!"

I covered my head. Oh, I'm too fond of my fur!

ZOOOOOOOmmm!!

A strange flying machine missed me by a whisker!

Holey cheese, Winglet was the pilot!

I ended up with four paws in the air as I dodged to avoid it. The empress landed in a cloud of **dust**. "Sorry, Knight! I'm still learning to fly these special machines from the Kingdom of Aircraft. This is the Floating Beetle — it's powered by pedals!"

"By pedal propulsion, to be exact!" a voice above us chimed in.

The sky darkened for a moment, covered by the wings of a royal **Emerald Dragon**.

It was my friend Lorian, the dragon tamer, seated on his faithful Narek!

"The Annoying One is here," Winglet said to me with a playful smile.

Those two were always bickering! But behind it all, they respected and loved each other.

LORIAN greeted me in his calm, confident voice. "Knight, I hope you had a good journey. We've been eagerly awaiting you!"

"It's an honor to see you again, my friend," I said solemnly.

I met Lorian on my last adventure, and he had been key to the success of our mission. He had PROTECTED Winglet every step of the way, facing thousands of dangers.

They teased each other all the time, but it was

easy to see they only had eyes for each other. Their **hearts** were as mushy as soft Brie!

"You're always playing my shadow!" Winglet said to him now.

He replied calmly, "You may be the empress, Winglet, but my duty will always be to protect you."

"And when the moment comes to **fight**, will you shut me up in a tower at Crystal Castle?" Winglet asked. "How will I defend my people from those who would destroy them if I can't take any risks?"

Wait one whisker-licking minute! Who wanted to destroy them? My whiskers trembled with fear as I asked, "Empress Winglet, who wants to destroy the empire? The CROWN has been recovered and good has returned to your lands, as the legends foretold."

Winglet murmured, "Yes, my friend. We thought we had won the fight against evil . . . but we were wrong! In spite of what the legends said, something didn't work. The Kingdom of Swamp Valley didn't disappear, and it hasn't transformed into the Kingdom of Blossom Valley!"

I turned as pale as a slab of mozzarella. The Kingdom of Swamp Valley was a dark, gloomy, evil land. It was defended by countless armed warriors:

Winglet looked at me intently. "If the empire hasn't been fully reunited, it means that the Kingdom of Swamp Valley is still a greater threat than we feared. If we don't find a way to stop it, it will attack us again. We'll be reduced to **nothing**!"

A SHADOW OVER THE EMPIRE

Holy cheese, I couldn't believe my ears!

My whiskers drooped. We had faced so many dangers and fought so hard to reunite the empire, and now it was in danger of DISAPPEARING forever?

"We need your help, Knight! More than ever before," Winglet said.

The empress scanned the horizon and said, "You arrived at just the right moment. We need your help to **DEFEAT** the Kingdom of Swamp Valley once and for all. We must not give in!"

I took a deep breath, even though I was shaking in my fur. "You can count on me, Empress!"

Winglet took my paw. "Thank you, brave Knight. We fought the Kingdom of Swamp Valley once, and we can do it again! Come with us to

Crystal Castle. Let's put our heads together and make a plan!"

We set off at once. When I saw Crystal Castle sparkling on the horizon, I felt my whole body, from whiskers to paws, fill with courage. I was so excited to be on my way to see Blossom, the Queen of the Fairies, again. She is a very good friend, and I have missed her.

As soon as I stepped foot inside Crystal Castle, I looked around for Blossom. Instead, we were greeted by a man with a **mustache** so long it reached the ground. He ran up to us with a notepad and quill in hand.

It was Professor Barnaby Grumbledon!

I had met him during our last adventure, when the Invisible Army had infiltrated Crystal Castle.

He cried, "We've been waiting for you!"

Winglet got straight to the point. "Professor Grumbledon, do you know how to **STOP** the Kingdom of Swamp Valley?"

"We're working on it, ztudying night and day, but

We've been waiting for you!

30

the zolution eludez uz! We must act immediately, before it'z too late! Follow me: My group of expertz in Ztrange Phenomena, Disappearancez, Abzurd Epizodez, and the Unexplained will update us on the zituation!"

Together, we headed to a gigantic hall with a huge door. In front of the door, a group of scholars was deep in conversation.

Winglet made the introductions. "These are our *court advisors*: the eminent Professor Digby McMouseford, Professor Yates Romano III, and Professor Niles Slice."

"It's a pleasure!" they said together, bowing one after another.

The first in line whispered with Professor Grumbledon.

"How? What? Zpeak louder!" Professor Grumbledon said, putting a **magnifying glass** to his ear.

The Court Advisors

I couldn't understand a cheese crumb of what they were saying, but I guessed that it wasn't good **NEWS**.

Grumbledon confirmed my suspicions. "They've consulted all the experts and all the books written on the subject, but we don't have a solution. Come

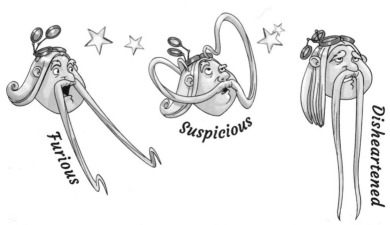

Furious

Suspicious

Disheartened

with me to the Empire Map Room!"

We followed behind him quickly. Cheese and crackers, what an incredible place! The room was completely packed with **maps**!

A small man in glasses ran here and there, saying to the cartographers, "Quick, quick! Draw, and don't stop!"

The empire seemed endless, so I imagined that drawing it all required sticking one piece of map here, another there, another up there, another down there. It was a never-ending job!

Winglet explained, "The Empire of Fantasy is being re-created as we speak. It's so big that every day new KINGDOMS join. Our mapmakers are constantly working to keep up!"

Just then the small man in glasses cried, "Add the Chocolate County to the west of the Kingdom of Ogres and to the east of the Kingdom of Toys!"

A rolled-up piece of paper popped out of

a tube sticking out of the wall. Squeak, it was a drawing of the Chocolate County!

One of the mapmakers snatched it and began to draw the map on a piece of parchment, then attached it to the grand map of the empire. This was an operation of fabumouse beauty!

But in the middle I could see a spot the color of ash, mud, and mold: **The Kingdom of Swamp Valley!**

Grumbledon sighed. "That's our problem, right there! We must find a way to stop it, or all the beauty you see here will disappear."

Winglet looked determined. "If we don't find a solution here, I'll go to the source of the problem: the Kingdom of Swamp Valley."

Just then *Queen Blossom* entered the room. How mousetastically wonderful to see her!

She looked at me with affection. "My dear Knight, we've missed you!"

Then she turned to Winglet, **worried**. "My daughter, don't be reckless. You cannot go to Swamp Valley. It is too dangerous!"

But Winglet wouldn't budge. "We can't just stay here and wait for the Invisible Army to return and **ATTACK**! We must act!"

Blossom replied, "You're going to run toward danger without knowing what awaits you? I

You cannot go!

admire your determination, my daughter. But you know that a true empress must show not only courage, but **wisdom** and patience, too."

"We've already waited too long!" Winglet cried. "I know that you want to protect me, but I've made my decision. Ruling an empire is not simple. Have faith in me. I must go — this is my **MISSION**!"

She grabbed her bow and arrows, leaped onto Dawn's back, and rushed out of the room before anyone could even squeak!

"Winglet!" Blossom called out to stop her.

Chattering cheddar, I couldn't allow the empress to go to such a dangerous place alone!

In the twitch of a whisker, Lorian and I took off after her.

I cried after Winglet, "Wait for us!" But she had already *SPED OFF* through the hallways of Crystal Castle.

As I tried to follow her, I tripped on my own

tail, did a somersault, tumbled forward, flew through the air at high speed, and landed like a flying wheel of cheese . . . right on Dawn's tail!

The tiger didn't seem too happy about that, but at least I had managed to catch up to Winglet!

"Knight," the empress said, turning to face me, "I must go! I must do it to **SAVE** our people, or the consequences will be terrible. Only you are capable of helping me on this **mission**. But if you don't want to follow me, I'll understand."

I sighed. "Truly, I . . ."

Just the thought of going into the lair of those **wicked** creatures gave me goose bumps — but I couldn't let my friend go straight into their clutches all alone!

"I . . . I will go with you!" I declared.

Lorian smiled at Winglet. "I won't let you fight them alone, either."

Winglet gazed at him and blushed. "Thank you, Lorian."

Then she turned to me. "I don't know how to thank you, Knight. When we return, I'll create a statue in your honor!"

Squeak, would the statue look as **TERRIFIED** as I felt?!

"Now let's go!" Winglet declared. "I'm sure that, together, we can do this!"

I hoped she was right.

But there was no time to think too much about it. We had to leave right away for the Rebel Empress's first mission!

A NEW MISSION

THE LAND
OF BOOKS

I flew along with Lorian on Narek's back. We were so high up that Winglet and Dawn looked tiny down below us!

There was just one teeny problem: I'm afraid of **HEIGHTS**! Luckily, a moment before we left, Winglet had made me put on the same special protective garments that I had worn on my first journey to the Empire of Fantasy. But would they protect me if I tumbled off the back of a flying dragon? *Squeak!*

Whiskers trembling, I tried not to look down. It was impawssible! When I did look, the COUNTRYSIDE was so beautiful it almost made me feel calm.

We flew over endless fields full of silver gazelles, forests filled with trees of every color, towns, cities, glaciers dotted with plumes of fire, and stretches of land that rippled like ocean waves. It was amazing how different all the lands of the **EMPIRE** were! Perhaps with a bit of luck, there would be a Kingdom of Gorgonzola or City of Sliced Cheddar somewhere out there. A mouse could dream, right?

I was lost in these sweet fantasies when Lorian said, "We're about to land! Down there, beyond that wood, is the final kingdom before the **Kingdom of Swamp Valley**. Hold on tight, Knight!"

With the wind ruffling my fur, I squeaked, "I'm already holding on tiiiiiiiiiiiiiiiiiiiiiiiiiiiiight!"

Slimy Swiss cheese! At this speed, we'd end up flattened on the ground like Parmesan pancakes!

Luckily, Lorian slowed us down in time, and Narek landed as light as a LEAF. Whew!

Winglet caught up to us after a moment. "Now,

we have to be careful. We don't know what awaits us within the borders of Swamp Valley!"

I raised a paw timidly and asked, "Empress . . . do we have a PLAN?"

"No, not really," my friend said. "But we'll have one soon. Follow me!"

No plan? **No plan?!** Why, oh why, did these things always happen to me?

Fear was making my fur stand on end. Suddenly, a familiar scent reached my snout. How delicious!

A voice shouted, "I'm late, I'm late!"

It was coming from a white rabbit bouncing around like a spring! He was wearing a vest and kept looking at a large **pocket watch** in his paw. He seemed to be in a big hurry! But where had I seen him before?

A moment later, a girl with long blonde hair ran after the

rabbit! She looked familiar to me, too . . . but why?

"All for one, one for all!"

Putrid cheese puffs! Who had shouted that?

Just then four knights in tunics and plumed hats jumped out from behind a bush! They reminded me of . . .

Oh, of course! How had I not known right away? It was the THREE MUSKETEERS and D'Artagnan*!

*They are the main characters in *The Three Musketeers* by Alexandre Dumas.

The answers to the games are on page 283.

So the rabbit with the watch was the White Rabbit! And the girl following him was Alice in Wonderland*!

Holey cheese, it seemed too good to be true! The main characters from some of the best **BOOKS** of all time had come to life right in front of me!

Lorian gallantly turned to the musketeers, who had crossed their swords right beneath my snout. "Musketeers, if it wouldn't trouble you too much, could you lower your **SHARP** blades?"

"Oh, pardon us!" D'Artagnan said. "We're always on guard. And you are . . . ?"

At the sight of Winglet, they all brightened and bowed.

"Empress, please excuse the rude greeting," D'Artagnan said with a bow. "It is a profound honor for us to have you here in the **LAND OF BOOKS**!"

---

*These are characters from *Alice's Adventures in Wonderland* by Lewis Carroll.

"The Land of Books?!" I squeaked happily.

"Of course!" Alice said with a smile. "The Land of Books is where the characters from the greatest stories live. If you hurry, you can have tea with the Mad Hatter and the March Hare!"

"Is this like the Land of Fairy Tales?" I asked, remembering the beautiful land I'd visited in my second journey to the Kingdom of Fantasy.

"Not exactly," replied the musketeer Aramis. "The characters in fairy tales are our cousins. We are **characters** from novels and plays."

My dear rodent friends, have you ever heard the phrase *library rat*? Well, that's me! I adore reading. More often than not, you can find me with my snout in the pages of a good book. Chattering cheddar, that must be where the wonderful scent was coming from. It was the smell of **BOOKS**!

Whiskers wobbling with excitement, I asked, "Then you must know the March sisters from *Little Women*?"

"Yes, and that's not all!" cried a young man, jumping down from a tree.

Winglet looked at him with **admiration**. "Robin Hood*! My idol!"

"In the flesh, mademoiselle," said Robin Hood, bowing to kiss her hand.

"Wow," Winglet said, sighing. She gave him an

*The main character of *The Merry Adventures of Robin Hood* by Howard Pyle adoring look. "You are the reason I even learned to use a **bow**!"

"Admire as you wish, mademoiselle," the archer said, and pulled up a blade of grass. He tossed it into the air, fired an arrow, and hit it perfectly!

"There you are, mademoiselle," he said, handing Winglet the blade of grass with a deep bow.

For you, mademoiselle!

"Ahem!" Lorian muttered, clearing his throat. "We have some urgent matters to take care of!"

I think my friend was a bit **JEALOUS**!

Winglet took Lorian by the hand. "Lorian means to say that we have an important **mission** to complete. We must go to Swamp Valley to see what is happening there," she explained.

"According to an ancient legend, when the empire is reborn, the Kingdom of Swamp Valley will be transformed into the Kingdom of Blossom Valley. Instead, something **dark** is happening. And we must find out what it is."

D'Artagnan, Alice, the White Rabbit, the three musketeers, and Robin Hood looked at us **FEARFULLY**.

"The empress is talking about . . . *that*!" Robin Hood said quietly, losing his confidence quickly.

"I'm also afraid she's referring to *that*," D'Artagnan murmured with a worried expression.

"It's terrible!" Alice sighed.

"I'm late, I'm late!" the White Rabbit cried.

Cheesy creampuffs, what was going on?

It seemed that these famouse characters were all afraid of something. I didn't know why, but I could almost feel the ground shake beneath my paws.

Winglet grew alarmed. "What are you talking about?"

"Follow us, and you'll see with your own eyes!" Alice said.

SUSPENSE

We continued into the heart of the **LAND OF BOOKS**, accompanied by our new friends. I couldn't seem to figure out what was worrying them. This place was truly marvemouse!

We passed a mountain as white as Dawn's fur, which rose up from the pages of a gigantic book. Above the peak, a herd of majestic **DRAGONS** fluttered, while on its slopes enchanted rocks glistened and waterfalls sparkled.

"That's Fantasy Novel Peak," Robin Hood explained.

Narek spewed a **FLAME** of excitement into the sky.

"That's his favorite kind of book!" Lorian said.

"Over there is the Tomb of Boredom and Slow Tomes," Robin added, nodding at an imposing monument supported by columns of thick books.

"And that's his favorite!" Winglet joked, ruffling Lorian's hair.

"Those are important books," he replied, crossing his arms. If you asked me, he still seemed a bit jealous!

We continued along a winding path with a panoramic view, which twisted and turned over pages that smelled like **roses**. "This is Love Story Overlook," Robin Hood murmured, giving Winglet a wink.

At last, we walked by a rusty and sinister-looking gate that was guarded by a creature with a threatening **SNEER**.

"That's Sinister Horror Village," Athos the musketeer explained.

We were just heading toward the Mystery Novel Suburbs when I thought I smelled something strange. Rats! The delightful fragrance of printed pages had disappeared!

Now there was a smell of **MOLD** . . . of dampness . . . of **rotting** pages!

"I'm late, I'm laaaaaate!" the White Rabbit squealed.

I turned to him. "Um, excuse me, but what are you late for?"

"For getting out of here quick as can be!" the White Rabbit squealed in panic.

Alice sighed, looking **FRIGHTENED**. "It's over there, at the border of the Land of Books!"

Then they all began talking at once.

"It froths . . ."

"It spreads . . ."

"It slips in . . ."

"It expands . . ."

"Slowly . . ."

"Relentlessly . . ."

But who were they talking about?

Or . . . what?

I couldn't put a paw on it!

Finally, I squeaked, "What are you talking about?"

"Forgive us," D'Artagnan said. "We're fictional characters — we like suspense! Its smell is unmistakable; its advance is unstoppable. Even now, it's on its way:

THE GREAT GRAYNESS!"

THE GREAT GRAYNESS

On the horizon, a cloud advanced toward us, creeping in like FOG, frothing like foam. It was as enormouse as a cloud of dust surrounding an invisible giant!

It seemed as though the Kingdom of Swamp Valley's wickedness was so powerful that it could overflow its borders, like the smoke rising from a potion in a witch's cauldron. As it passed, everything withered: Flowers wilted, book pages molded, colors faded, birds went silent, wooden doors rotted, walls flaked away, roofs caved in, and everything was covered in a moldy layer of disgusting ooze.

But worst of all, the story characters in its path turned gray, sad, and worried, just like the inhabitants of the **Kingdom of Swamp Valley**!

We saw a queen, gray from the top of her crown to the hem of her cloak. She walked in circles with an absentminded look on her face, dragging a scepter with a **BROKEN** heart at the top.

How terrible!

"Oh no!" said the White Rabbit. "Even the Queen of Hearts has been struck by the **GREAT GRAYNESS**! The most beautiful pages of *Alice's Adventures in Wonderland* have been ruined, destroyed, and spoiled like rotten carrots!"

"And down there is *The Wonderful Wizard of Oz's* Emerald City," Robin Hood explained, pointing to a **crumbling** castle. "Once upon a time, it sparkled as

green as your dragon's scales," he said to Lorian, "but now it's grayer than a **mud puddle**."

Narek nosed at the dragon tamer, letting a puff of smoke out of his nostrils. I could tell he didn't like the idea of turning that **muddy** color at all!

Lorian petted him fondly and reassured him, "Don't worry, my friend! We'll stay away from that evil cloud."

"Look over there," Winglet said quietly. She was pointing

to a skinny gray boy who was sprawled out, motionless, on a branch.

A tiny fairy fluttered around him. She was also gray, disheveled, and . . .

Holey cheese! I could hardly squeak — that was Peter Pan and Tinker Bell*!

"Oh no," I murmured. "They've been struck by the Great Grayness, too!"

Winglet hugged me. "Does this mean that the WICKEDNESS that rules Swamp Valley is seeping into the Land of Books?"

"Yes, My Empress," Robin Hood said gravely. "Our world is at risk of being destroyed forever!"

"Entire regions on the border of the Kingdom of Swamp Valley have already been damaged,"

*The main characters of *Peter Pan* by J. M. Barrie

D'Artagnan added. "Look!"

He pointed his sword at the horizon. We could see field after field **devastated** by the Great Grayness!

Slimy Swiss balls! This danger was getting closer and more threatening by the minute. There was no time to waste!

"**HELP, HELP!**" a voice shouted.

It was a young girl. She looked like she was trying to escape, but she had gotten tangled in a bramble.

THE GRAYNESS WAS CREEPING UP ON HER!

"That's Anne, the main character of Lucy Maud Montgomery's book *Anne of Green Gables*!" Alice explained.

"Poor thing!" I shouted, heading toward her as

fast as my paws would take me. "Quick, we have to free her immediately!"

We ran to help her, but as Lorian tried to help Anne to her feet, something strange happened . . .

A gray *gust of air* surrounded the three musketeers and D'Artagnan! It reached out toward us, too, but missed by a whisker.

Everyone for themselves!

"Bah!" D'Artagnan grumbled, leaving poor Anne to her fate. "One for all . . . and everyone for themselves!"

"You said it!" the three musketeers replied, each heading off in his own direction.

Even Robin Hood walked away, muttering, "Stealing from the rich to give to the poor? I'd be better off just taking care of myself!"

"Noooo!" I cried.

My new friends had been struck by the Great Grayness! They had instantly become gloomy, selfish, angry, and GRAY. Rats!

Only Alice and the White Rabbit had stayed safe at our sides. Now what?

THE MOST EVIL
OF ALL

This marvemouse kingdom was in terrible danger! But how could we possibly fight against it?

"The problem is more serious than we feared," Winglet said, heartbroken. "The **Kingdom of Swamp Valley** has existed for hundreds and thousands of years, but it has never expanded beyond its borders before."

Lorian frowned. "As a wise person once said: 'Evil breeds more **evil**, unless someone stands in its way!' We can't let this continue."

Winglet nodded, looking determined. "You're right! We'll go to the Kingdom of Swamp Valley, and we'll stop the Great Grayness!"

"You are truly **courageous**," Alice said. "I would also like to go fight with you, but to tell you the truth, I always just seem to get in trouble."

"Don't worry, Alice," I said. "It's up to us to complete this MISSION!"

Just then we heard a voice singing softly . . . then squawking . . . then screeching like a rusty bicycle.

It was coming from the Adventure Novel Woods!

"Zin zan zee zumber,
Who disturbs my slumber?
Zan zoon zee zown,
Close your beak, pipe down!
Zun zan zee and zen,
I don't want to hear you again!"

"Who's there?" Winglet cried.

We peeked around a nearby tree and saw a witch swinging in a hammock.

She looked just like a regular **WITCH**, or at least like the ones I'd met in my journeys to the Kingdom of Fantasy. She had an evil sneer, long dark hair, and a wart on her nose. But her witch's hat was **CAPPED** with a crown, and instead of a broom, she had an **UMBRELLA**.

What strange accessories. Moldy mozzarella,

maybe I wasn't up
to date on the latest
witch trends!

"It was torture hearing
you heroes chatter on!" the
witch cackled. "You can save
your breath. The Great Grayness will **devour**
all of you! You're better off giving up. And now, if
you don't mind, I'd like to nap in peace!"

"That's the Wicked Witch

of the West," the White Rabbit whispered. "Ever since the magical Land of Oz was attacked by the Great Grayness, she hasn't been the same."

"More like the LAZY Witch of the West," a deep voice said. "She just lies around in that HAMMOCK all the time!"

We all turned in the direction of the voice. Thundering cattails, it was the ferocious, fearsome, unstoppable Captain Hook!

The Wicked Witch of the West grumbled, "Ha, ha, so says the terror of the seven seas! At this point, you couldn't even FRIGHTEN a codfish. Ha, ha, ha!"

"Go on, laugh!" Captain Hook sneered. "You couldn't even scare Dorothy's brainless friend, the Scarecrow!"

"Well, your HOOK couldn't even be used for

skewering marshmallows!" the Witch of the West retorted.

"By Blackbeard's ghost!" Hook boomed. "How dare you? I am the most evil VILLAIN ever written!"

"Nice try — I'm much more evil than you!" The witch cackled and jumped out of her hammock, looking smug.

"Oh, really? I'll show you!" Hook challenged her.

He stepped toward the edge of a nearby lake where a group of kids were fishing, looking happy and peaceful.

Among them, I recognized a kid with a straw **hat** and rolled-up pants. It was Tom Sawyer, the hero of Mark Twain's book!

Holey cheese, how I had loved his **adventures**. I remembered them all from my childhood! I had spent hours and hours reading about him . . .

"Wait and see," said Hook. Then he shouted, "Come on, you scorpion fish! Who wants to try my hook?"

The kids looked up at him, were silent for a moment . . . then they burst out **LAUGHING**!

They all went back to fishing, as if a pesky gnat had flown by. Hook was shocked.

The Witch held her belly as she laughed. "Ha, ha, ha! Is that all you can do? Watch and learn, Hooky!"

She stretched her fingers out toward the kids, opened her eyes wide, and chanted, "Zan zee zo zere, the Wicked Witch of the West is here!"

Hook laughed so hard he could hardly catch his breath. "Ha, ha, ha! Who do you think you're going to scare with that ridiculous nursery rhyme?"

But the kids stared at the witch. Their jaws dropped with FEAR . . . and they ran away!

"Ha, ha, ha! See? What did I tell you, you swashbuckling fool?" the witch bragged.

"I'm the one they were afraid of!" Hook replied stubbornly.

As they continued to argue over who was scarier, an immense shadow blocked out the sky. Just looking at it filled my heart with dismay. There was no question . . .

IT WAS THE GREAT GRAYNESS!

So that was what had **terrified** the kids, not the Wicked Witch of the West!

"Help!" the witch shouted.

"Holy flying squid!" cried Captain Hook.

In a moment of terror, the wicked pair c**clung** to each other, shaking in terror. Great Gorgonzola! Who would have ever imagined a scene like that?

The cloud passed slowly, leaving us all with feelings of anxiety, deep sadness, and horror. Hook and the Witch of the West quickly separated, **RED** with embarrassment.

Winglet peered at them closely. "Can you explain what's going on?"

The pair looked defeated.

"Oh, all right!" the Witch of the West said with a sigh.

"I'll start," said Captain Hook. "Once upon a time here in the Land of Books, we were the most respected villains . . ."

"Everyone feared us!" the witch interjected. "From the smallest characters to the largest, no one dared even breathe when we appeared!"

"Those were the days," Hook commented wistfully. "But things have changed. Ever since the Great Grayness began seeping out of the Kingdom of Swamp Valley, our **WICKEDNESS** isn't frightening to anyone. They're all afraid of turning gray. Now our threats just seem like jokes!"

Cheese niblets! The Great Grayness really was an unparalleled evil!

The Witch of the West confessed, "Compared

to the wickedness coming from Swamp Valley, we're just beginners. We can't **scare** anyone anymore. That's why I'm always lying around in my hammock. What's the point?"

Hook put an arm around her shoulders. "We've been outdone. We're old news. And in the end, the **GRAYNESS** will take us, too!"

As the Wicked Witch and Captain Hook both began to sob miserably, Winglet's voice rang out as crystal clear as ever. "Don't say that! You can't give up. If we join forces, we can fight this!"

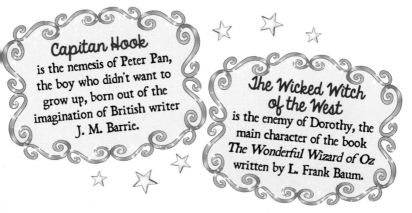

Capitan Hook is the nemesis of Peter Pan, the boy who didn't want to grow up, born out of the imagination of British writer J. M. Barrie.

The Wicked Witch of the West is the enemy of Dorothy, the main character of the book *The Wonderful Wizard of Oz* written by L. Frank Baum.

THE HOOK . . .
AND THE UMBRELLA!

"What?" the Wicked Witch of the West cried.

"Huh?" Hook echoed.

"How?" Alice, the White Rabbit, and I chorused.

"Us? You mean us?" Hook and the Wicked Witch asked.

"Yes, you!" Winglet said. "You could join us! If we defeat the Great Grayness, it will save your world and also make you even more terrifying and intimidating. You mustn't lose faith in yourselves!"

Lorian and I looked at each other in shock. The evilest villains from literature were going to join us? Of all the strange ideas I'd heard, this was the strangest of all!

But the empress knew what she was doing. We trusted her!

Winglet continued. "I'm sure that you would be unbeatable against the Invisible Army. After all, who could be more prepared to fight **evil** than the evilest villains of all?"

A glimmer appeared in Captain Hook's eyes, and it wasn't just the reflection of his hook. It was a glimmer of determination!

The Wicked Witch's **HAT** also seemed to glow with fierceness!

Hook said, "I suppose the empress is right. We can regain our reputations as great villains!"

The witch grinned. "For once I'll admit that you're right, you rusty skewer! This can't be the end of our cruelty, our superior wickedness, or our despicable ruthlessness!"

"This is our moment of redemption!" Hook cheered.

Lorian gave Winglet a worried look. "Um,

are you sure this is the right move?"

"Positive," said Winglet.

Squeak! I really, really, *really* hoped that our *empress* was correct!

"To be honest," said the Wicked Witch, "ever since little Dorothy was struck by the Great Grayness, I haven't had any fun!"

Hook nodded. "Yes! When Peter Pan turned into a lazy, grumpy old slipper, life became a total bore."

"If the Great Grayness wins, the Emerald City will never sparkle again," the Wicked Witch said with a sigh, "and it won't be any fun to attack it!"

"If we don't FIGHT the Great Grayness, Neverland will no longer exist!" said Hook.

"But if it's called Neverland," the witch wondered aloud, "how does it even exist in the first place?"

Captain Hook scratched his head with his hook, then said, "Don't think about it so hard!"

He crossed his sword with the tip of the witch's umbrella as a symbol of their   .

Winglet smiled. "And so a new friendship is born!"

"Let's not exaggerate," the Wicked Witch cackled. "We'll just call it a little suspension of DISLIKE!"

·Hook nodded. "Exactly! Once we return from this mission, I will go back to being a thorn in your side. But for now, we are allies!" He thought for a moment. "I will even take a break from picking fights with my biggest enemy, CROCODILE! I'm afraid there's no chance he'll be able to outrun the Great Grayness."

Winglet said, "Yes! And don't worry, if we have anything to say about it, the Great Grayness's minutes are numbered."

"If the Great Grayness keeps moving at this speed, we're the ones whose minutes are numbered," the White Rabbit said anxiously.

"How many minutes?" Winglet asked.

The rabbit consulted his pocket watch. "If we skip our naps and tea, exactly three thousand, one

hundred and twenty minutes, thirty seconds, and six milliseconds."

Lorian did a quick mental calculation and said, "That's just about **two days and four hours**."

My eyes were as round as wheels of cheese.

"The **FASTEST** way to reach our destination is to sail along Happy Reading River," Captain Hook said. "It flows to the border of the Kingdom of Swamp Valley, then turns into the muddy Boredom River. I'm an expert in navigation. We can even use my **ship**!"

"Your tub, you mean," the Wicked Witch cackled.

Captain Hook bristled. "My glorious ship is perhaps a bit rusty, but it's still a ship! Come on, crew! We must retrieve my ship from the **bottom of the sea!**"

HEAVE-HO!

hundering cattails!

When we reached Fishbone Bay, it was clear that the ship was more than a little **rusty**. It looked like an enormouse boulder covered in mollusks, barnacles, clams, and mussels! It had been stranded on the bottom of the bay for so long that a layer of SEAWEED covered it like a cloak . . .

It was so buried in the sand that only the prow* stuck out above the surface of the water . . .

And it was so grim and gloomy that there was just one figurehead** on the prow — a **SKULL**! Rats!

Seaweed had stuck to the skull in the shape of a mustache, and a clam had settled right on top of its head. So, strangely, it didn't scare me at all!

"My faithful ship just needs a little tune-up and

*The prow is the area at the front of the ship.
**The figurehead is the wooden sculpture that decorates the prow of a ship.

she'll be as good as new!" Captain Hook said.

The Witch of the West **cackled** in his face. "Sure, but how are you going to get it to float again? Maybe I should just float on a pool noodle instead?"

"You could try something other than chattering, you old crone!" Hook said. He grabbed a thick rope tied to the ship and said, "Something useful, maybe. Follow the lead of this **FEARLESS KNIGHT** here. As you can see, he's as sharp as

fresh cheddar! Here you go, Knight!"

He tossed the 𝓇𝓄𝓅ℯ to me.

I **leaped** up to grab it like a fish . . .

. . . but missed! My paws crossed, and I tumbled forward.

Oops!

Argh!

SPLASH!

I landed snoutfirst in the water with a tremendmouse splash! I looked like such a **cheesebrain**!

"Grab on!" Captain

Hook said, reaching his hook out to me.

I grabbed it, feeling like a fish on a fishhook, and was pulled back onto dry land. *Squeak!*

"Now we'll hoist up the **ship**," Hook said, not missing a beat.

"Together, we can do it!" Winglet cried. Alice and the White Rabbit got ready to help, too.

Holding the rope like we were about to play a game of tug-of-war, we all began to pull together.

HEAVE-HO!

HEAVE-HO!

HEAVE-HO!

I was exhausted . . . and the ship had moved only one little inch!

It was enormousely heavy!

Luckily, Narek was on our side. Thanks to his **dragon** mega-muscles, we managed to pull

How terrifying!

up the ship little by little until the whole thing had finally surfaced.

"Hooray!"

we cheered.

"We did it!" Winglet cried, satisfied. "This ship is perfect!"

The ship looked just like a pirate ship should, with a ripped **flag**, torn sails, and a gangplank for jumping into the water and becoming shark bait.

Crusty cat litter! I hoped I didn't end up on that gangplank!

"Ha, ha, ha, it's quite the wreck!" the Wicked Witch sneered at Captain Hook, enjoying herself.

"No, no, it will be just right for our mission," said Winglet. "It's dark enough to let us slip into **SWAMP VALLEY** unseen, and it will give us the chance to investigate without anyone noticing!"

Lorian looked worried. "Yes, but speaking of the Great Grayness . . . how will we sail right into the heart of the Kingdom of Swamp Valley without touching any of it?"

Winglet sighed. "That's a real problem."

We couldn't escape the Great Grayness, could we?

How?

Rotten rat's teeth, what a problem!

Before we could even leave for the Kingdom of Swamp Valley, it seemed like our mission had hit a wall!

THE FREE WISH

We had our ship, but we still didn't know what to do about the Great Grayness.

"Oh, I know!" cried the Witch of the West.

Everyone turned to her hopefully.

She grinned. "We'll use my HAT, with all of its precious jewels!"

"How is that going to help us?" Winglet asked.

The Wicked Witch explained, "In the book *The Wonderful Wizard of Oz*, the hat allows me to grant *three wishes*. Long ago, when I was cleaning my attic, I discovered that I still had the bag from the magical shop where I'd bought it. Inside that bag was a voucher for a fRee wish, only for the most important customers!"

She rummaged around in her pockets. "Now where did I put it? Ah, here it is!"

She pulled out a crinkled **piece of paper**.

"I've been saving it for just the right occasion," the witch continued.

She placed the voucher in my paw. After I'd read it, I asked, "Forgive me, Witch of the West, but it says here it's good for one mini wish. What does that mean?"

The Perfect Witch
WITH OUR COMPLIMENTS!
1 FREE MINI WISH!

"Oh!" She sighed. "I've already made the three bigger wishes: The first was used to conquer the land of the Winkies, the SECOND was used to drive away the Wizard of Oz, and the third was to attack Dorothy and her annoying friends with my flying monkeys. So I can't ask for anything big, like defeating the Invisible Army, saving the empire, or making Hook scary for once . . ."

Captain Hook grumbled, "At the end of this adventure, I'll make you pay for all your nonsense, or I'm not the terror of the seven seas!"

The witch added, "But . . . I think I *could* make our company immune to the Great Grayness! Come gather around me!" she called. "It's time for . . .

THE WITCH'S ENCHANTMENT!"

Double twisted rat tails! How terrifying!

Alice looked at the White Rabbit. "It's time for us to go. We wish you success in your mission to bring PeACe to the Land of Books! We will wait in the White Rabbit's den. We'll be safe there!"

We waved good-bye to our new friends, and then Winglet, Lorian, Dawn, Narek, Captain Hook, and I formed a circle around the Wicked Witch of the West. She pulled her hat all the way down to her nose and began the spell.

She started to **SKIP** around, then took a wooden spoon and a dented can out of her pocket, and began to smack the spoon against the can. (How moustastically strange!)

At last, she began to chant her spell.

"Zin zan zee zay,
Ugly Grayness, go away!
Zan zon zin zon,
Sadness and boredom, both be gone!
Zin zan zoon zus,
Stay far away from us!"

She paused, then murmured, "Strange, very strange . . . oh! What was I thinking? We're missing this!" She pulled a slipper out of her pocket, which she rotated three times above her head.

Suddenly, a bright **LIGHT** surrounded all of us!

MERLIN'S MAP

When the dazzling light disappeared, I checked my ears, snout, and paws. At least I had made it out in one piece — fur, whiskers, and all!

"The **spell** worked!" the Witch of the West cheered. "The Great Grayness will have no effect on us now, and we will be able to enter the Kingdom of Swamp Valley."

As far as I could tell, I looked exactly the same as before. I guess sometimes enchantments are INVISIBLE!

"Thanks to you, our first problem is solved," Winglet said with a smile. "Now we need to face the second one: figuring out exactly how to get to the Kingdom of Swamp Valley."

"We need a MAP," said Captain Hook. "Just

like the maps that have led me to some of the greatest treasures! Ah, I remember when —"

"This isn't the time for your boring trips down memory lane!" the Witch of the West interrupted. "Get those *gears turning* and come up with an idea!"

Suddenly, Hook snapped his fingers. "I've got it — we could ask the wizard Merlin for help! Surely that old bearded fellow has something that could help us."

How fabumouse! I would get to visit again with Merlin*, the **wizard** from the legends of King Arthur.

"The problem is that he'll never let us into his workshop," Captain Hook said. "That wizard is as stubborn and tough as whalebone!"

Winglet declared, "Let's go to him anyway

*I met Merlin in my first *Journey Through Time*.

and see what happens. I'm sure that he can be persuaded to help. Lead the way, Captain!"

Merlin's **HOUSE** was located in the Cave of Ancient Legends, on the slopes of Fantasy Novel Peak.

When we arrived, Merlin stood in front of his front door, waving his *magic wand* up and down as a frog jumped around.

"**OH NO!**" Merlin cried. "Once again, my Anti-Grayness Spell didn't work!"

"Hello, Merlin," Winglet greeted him.

"Empress," the wizard said with a bow. "How delightful to see you! I was just trying to create a spell to reverse the **EFFECTS** of the Grayness, but I still need to work on it a bit more . . ."

The frog protested, "CROAK, CROAK, CROAK?! CROAK, CROAK, CROAK, CROAK, CROAK, CROAK, CROAK, CROAK!*"

"Oh," said Merlin, "my friend is a little oversensitive! But what brings you to my home?"

Winglet's voice broke as she spoke. "We must make a journey to Swamp Valley to figure out

* Translation from ancient Frogese: "Just a bit?! Look what you've done to the great and powerful fairy Morgana!"

where the Great Grayness is coming from and stop it at its source. We need a map to **guide** us there, and we thought maybe you could help!"

Merlin murmured, "Even my dear Arthur has been struck by the Grayness . . . as well as my friend Morgana, though she had a **bad attitude** even before this, so it's not a huge difference . . ."

"CROAK, CROAK, CROAK, CROAK!*"

Merlin continued. "As I was saying, let me think. I must have a map around here! I'm sure it's here somewhere. Wait just a minute!"

Quick as a flash, he disappeared into his mysterious workshop.

For a while, we heard him rummaging around.

"I thought I had put it here . . ."

BANG! CRASH! OOF!

*Translation from ancient Frogese: "I heard that, you old kettle!"

"Everything okay in there?" Winglet called.

Merlin stepped back outside with his hat askew. "Unfortunately, I can't figure out where I put that map. But I found some other objects that might be useful for your journey: a travel guide to the Kingdom of Swamp Valley and a very useful **ANTI-HUMIDITY KIT**. It has rubber boots, a mud-proof raincoat, and a girdle. Go on, try them, Knight!"

Before I could squeak, I found myself stuffed into a bone-squeezing **GIRDLE**.

Why do these things always happen to me?!

Girdle

Barely able to breathe, I murmured, "Thanks so much, Merlin, sir, but maybe we'd be better off with something that doesn't attract so much attention?"

"Perhaps if we all looked through your WORKSHOP together, we could find something more useful. Perhaps even the map," Lorian suggested.

"Impossible," Merlin replied. "**NO ONE**, and I mean **NO ONE**, goes into my workshop except for me. I'm always looking for things, so I'm an expert by now. If I didn't find it, it's because the map wasn't there! Are you trying to say that I'm wrong?"

"I told you he was as tough and stubborn as whalebone," Hook whispered to me.

Lorian tried again. "Of course — I didn't mean to offend you! I just meant to say that together we can overcome the greatest **difficulties**. After all, twelve eyes can see a lot more than two!"

Merlin frowned. "Just one of my eyes sees better than a hundred other eyes! But since you seem to disagree, I'll let you give it a try. Follow me!"

Merlin opened a door that led into a hallway. At the end was another small door, a bit narrower than the last, and a smaller hallway.

Then another smaller door, a smaller hallway, an even smaller door, and so on until the seventh tiny door, so narrow that I regretted taking off that girdle!

Slimy Swiss balls, how could such a small **house** contain all these hallways and doors?

At last, we reached Merlin's workshop.

"Shiver me timbers, this truly is a magical place!" Hook whistled with admiration.

"Let's start searching for the **map**," Lorian suggested.

Working together, we found the map in the twitch of a whisker! Hooray!

"Here it is!" the empress called from across the room.

The map had been hiding in plain sight, rolled up and tied with a red ribbon. Merlin simply hadn't spotted it!

When Winglet opened up the map, we noticed that there was a drawing on the back, but we weren't sure what it was. Maybe it was just a decorative design?

We rolled up the map up and put it in a safe place. Now that we had found the map of the Kingdom of Swamp Valley, the gloomiest place in the whole empire, all we had to do was return to Fishbone Bay and set sail!

The answers to the games are on page 283.

Maybe it's here?

GAME
Can you find the map
of the Kingdom of
Swamp Valley?

GRAYER THAN THE GRAY ONES!

The thought of encountering the Invisible Army again made my whiskers **tremble** with fright!

But I would face any mousely terror in order to help Winglet save the empire!

Trying not to seem like the soft cheese I really was, I took the **LEAD**. "Well, let's shake a tail! Thanks, Merlin!" I led the way, scampering back through the seven doors, seven long hallways, and finally outside.

I would walk **bravely** toward danger, to face an unknown destiny, and . . .

Hey! Why wasn't anyone following me?

"Um, Knight," said Lorian.

"Pardon me, but I think you're forgetting something!"

"Who? What?" I cried.

Hook rolled his eyes. "With that colorful outfit of yours, you'll stick out like a sore thumb in the middle of the gray Kingdom of Swamp Valley."

Winglet smiled. "Hook is right. It's not enough just to be immune to the Great Grayness. We also need to pass through Swamp Valley unseen!"

"I have just the thing!" Merlin cried. "A nice gray that will make you seem like true inhabitants of Swamp Valley. It's a magical color and is resistant to water, dragon flame, and natural disasters!"

I wasn't so sure about this. "But, Merlin, if it's really that resistant, how will we get it off once we come back?"

Merlin straightened the point of his hat. "Well, we can deal with that later, if you come back!"

IF?

Squeeeeek! I was going to be turned into mouse meatballs by the Invisible Army!

Merlin ran back to get a very, very, very big cauldron, which he dragged outside. It was full of a dense gray substance, sort of like mud. It had a **STRONG** smell!

Dawn, who had come up to investigate, roared with disgust.

"Come on, my dear tiger," Winglet urged her. "I know you don't want to give up your beautiful white coat, but we have to adapt. It's all part of our **MISSION**! We will get you back to normal in no time."

In the meantime, Merlin had gone back inside to look for something else.

The sound of dishes **BREAKING** came from inside the house. Then we heard a yelp.

Then came the sound of crockery crumbling, and another cry. "By my great-grandfather's beard! What miserable wizardry!"

Finally, we heard the sound of metal objects falling, and even more hollering. "Forgetful frogs! Where is that thing hiding?"

We were about to give up when Merlin popped back outside, holding a big **paintbrush**. He used it to mix up the goopy substance in the cauldron.

Bleck! What a terrible stink!

At last, with a tap of Merlin's magic wand, the paintbrush came to life . . . and started to paint us!

I also got a bucket of **COLOR** to the head! In the end, we were all gray from ears to toes. Not even my little nephew Benjamin would have been able to tell me apart from one of the residents of Swamp Valley!

"I'm all gray and **stinky**!" Captain Hook grumbled. "It reminds me of the time that old Peg Leg and I were spending the night at Piratetown Port, and the seagulls flying overhead gave us a horrible surprise!"

"Hook!" The Wicked Witch of the West shushed him. "Does this seem like the right time to tell your pointless stories? You're such a **stick-in-the-mud**!"

"Well, now that you're a completely gray witch, you're even less **TERRIFYING**!" the pirate replied with a sneer.

I sighed. Those two fought worse than cats and rats!

"I don't know how to thank you for your help, Merlin," Winglet said. "You're a true friend."

You're such a stick-in-the-mud!

The wizard looked at her very seriously. Rats, what had the empress said wrong?

When Merlin spoke, his voice was a warning. "In the Kingdom of Swamp Valley, you must be sure not to say nice things! Remember, that land is ruled by anger and sadness. And above all," the wizard added,

"YOU MUST NEVER, EVER, EVER SAY THE NINE POSITIVE WORDS DETAILED IN THE PARCHMENT OF POSITIVITY!"

"The Parchment of Positivity?!" we all repeated, confused.

Merlin nodded. "The *Parchment of Positivity* is posted in front of the gates of Swamp Valley. Because of an evil spell cast by the ancient wizard Hordus, the warlock who turned the Kingdom of Blossom Valley into the Kingdom of Swamp Valley, anyone there who says one of the positive words listed on the parchment will be condemned to a **terrible fate**!"

"Turned into one of the Invisibles?" Winglet guessed with a frown.

"Worse!" replied Merlin.

The Wicked Witch of the West asked, "Plastered in mud?"

"Much worse!"

I asked in a trembling voice, "D-d-death?"

"If only!"

Merlin remained silent for a few moments

before continuing in a dramatic tone. "They will be transformed into the only creatures more invisible than the Invisibles, those who will never become visible again: the SHAPELESS ONES!"

Merlin held up a finger. "However, of all the words on the Parchment of Positivity, only the ninTH gives a ray of hope. Saying this word turns you into a Shapeless One but allows you to become visible again. But no one has been able to figure out how!"

"I didn't know SHAPELESS ONES existed," Lorian said. "But what is the difference between them and the Invisibles?"

Merlin covered his face with his hands and sighed. "You don't even know the basics! The inhabitants of Swamp Valley are divided into three categories . . ."

With a tap of his magic wand, a large chalkboard appeared.

1) GRAY ONES=
sadness + anger + stress

These are the gray inhabitants of the Kingdom of Swamp Valley.

PRIMARY TASKS: complaining about living in Swamp Valley, sowing discord and anxiety as often as possible

2) INVISIBLE ARMY=
sadness + anger + stress + ability to appear and disappear

This is the army of the Kingdom of Swamp Valley.

PRIMARY TASKS: defending the Kingdom and destroying all that is good

3) SHAPELESS ONES=
eternal invisibility!

These are the enemies of the Kingdom of Swamp Valley, and as punishment, they are made permanently invisible, with no hope of ever reappearing. Through the ancient will of Hordus, anyone who has positive feelings in their heart must disappear instantly!

Merlin cleared his throat and began to read.

I wasn't sure I had understood everything, but I was sure of one thing: We absolutely must not be turned into SHAPELESS ONES!

"Off you go, my heroes," said Merlin, wringing his hands with nerves. "All I can do now is wish you good luck!"

"CROAK, CROAK, CROAK, CROAK!*" added Morgana.

"We won't disappoint you," Winglet said fiercely. "We'll bring happiness and color back to these lands!"

We returned to Captain Hook's **ship** and prepared to set sail for our dark and perilous destination.

Rancid ricotta, I was shaking in my fur!

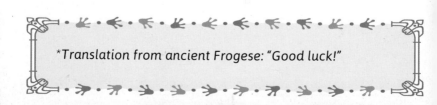

Translation from ancient Frogese: "Good luck!"

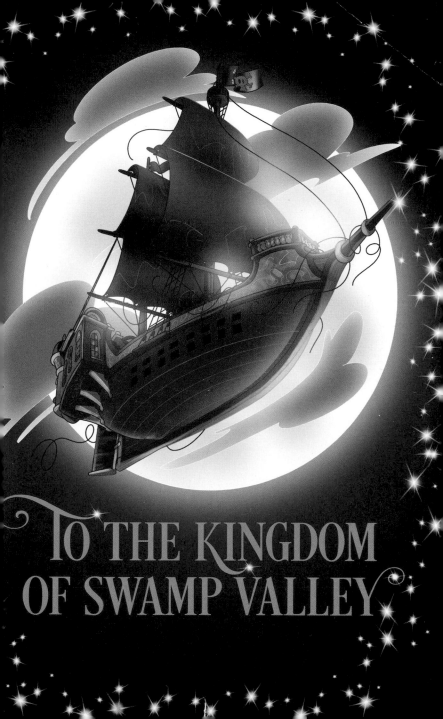

TO THE KINGDOM
OF SWAMP VALLEY

THE PARCHMENT OF POSITIVITY

From the Sea of Buccaneers, we sailed toward Happy Reading River. The river flowed calmly, rocking us with a gentle sway.

Colorful FISH leaped above the surface, and a light breeze ruffled my fur.

It seemed impawssible that these crystal waters would become the **muddy** River of Boredom!

As we approached the border of the Kingdom of Swamp Valley the ship started to slow down. The water had become as thick as cheese fondue!

"So that's why it's called the *River of Boredom*. It runs so slowly that we all might die of boredom!" the Witch of the West said.

All kinds of objects were bobbing on the surface: fish bones, old shoes, tin cans, rotten seaweed, apple cores, and pieces of things we couldn't identify.

Hook muttered, "Yarrr! This water looks like the slop that the ship's cook usually makes!"

The air grew **damp**, so much so that my whiskers wilted like clumps of seaweed. Holey cheese!

"And what a **stink**!" added the Wicked Witch of the West, holding her nose.

"We have to act like locals," said Winglet. "Don't

hold your noses, otherwise they'll recognize us as outsiders right away! We'll have to pretend that this is the most **delightful** fragrance, like it would be for any resident of Swamp Valley."

Crusty cat litter, this was going to be tough!

Suddenly, we could see a line of **SKULLS** and assorted **bones** along the riverbank. It must be the border between the Land of Books and the Kingdom of Swamp Valley . . .

And we were about to cross it! Rats!

"Look down there," said Lorian. "That must be the *parchment* Merlin was telling us about!"

A piece of parchment, curled and frayed from the humidity, was attached to a spear sticking out of the ground.

We could see what was written at the top: *Parchment of Positivity*. We leaned over the side to read the rest (after all, the ship was going sooooo slowly that we would have had time to take a nap!), but something wasn't right . . .

"Isn't there supposed to be a list of the words on there that we should NEVER, EVER, EVER say?" I asked, squinting. "I don't see it!"

Lorian studied the parchment carefully. "Strange, very strange. It looks like the letters have all been mixed up!"

"What could have happened?" a voice rang out.

Parchment of Positivity

Anyone who says one of these words in the land of the Kingdom of Swamp Valley will instantly be turned into a Shapeless One!

1)

2)

3)

4)

5)

6)

7)

8)

9)

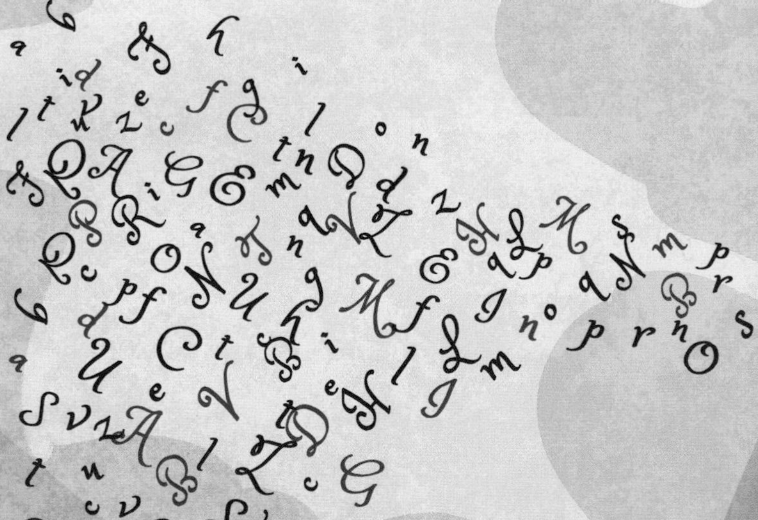

"Ha, ha! So many questions!"

I cupped my ears and cried, "What? Huh? Who was that?!"

At that moment, a strong *gust* of wind had ruffled my fur, made the Wicked Witch of the West's hat fly off (luckily, Lorian grabbed it before it fell into the muddy water), and almost knocked Winglet off balance. We looked around but didn't see anyone. Even Dawn and Narek seemed nervous. That mysterious voice seemed to be coming from **THIN AIR**!

Hook shook his hook in the air and shouted, "Walloping whalebones, who are you? Speak up, if you have the courage!"

The voice exhaled, blowing like wind through the trees on a stormy day.

"My name is Wickedious, and I confess,
Where I go, so goes the
Great Grayness.
With a foul, evil wind I've blown away
the words of joy, pleasure, and harmony.
For this band of heroes,
the adventure's just begun.
For soon, you'll be turned
into Shapeless Ones!"

Because of the evil wind, the positive words had been blown away. Only **scattered letters** remained!

"P-p-pardon me, Wickedious," I sputtered. "You mean to say that we won't know what these words are, and we might say them by mistake?"

The wind whistled cruelly,

"You are correct, little mousely one:

It's disaster for you, but for me it's good fun!"

Then it let out a fur-freezing cackle and disappeared. It had vanished, just like the positive words it had *blown* away!

My whiskers were wobbling out of control!

Lorian put an encouraging hand on my shoulder. "I'm afraid that our journey will be even more dangerous than we thought, my noble friend. We must be very careful about how we speak."

"Or we'll disappear forever!"

Captain Hook thundered after a dramatic pause. "Forgive me. In addition to suspense, we fictional characters love climactic scenes!"

Holey cheese, if this was how our journey was beginning, how much worse could it get?

Squeeeeeeak!

The wind, Wickedious, blew away the words that you must NEVER, EVER say aloud in the Kingdom of Swamp Valley . . . otherwise, you'll turn into a Shapeless One! Can our heroes learn what the words are?

Figure it out with them during the adventure. They are marked by this symbol: ♡. Get a piece of paper and write them down for yourself! You can find all the words on the

Parchment of Positivity at the end of the book.

See if you can discover what the ninth word is: the most positive word of all!

This is the only word that will keep you from remaining a Shapeless One for all time . . . if you manage to break the enchantment.

THE RIVER OF BOREDOM

After hearing this gloomy news, we continued down the River of Boredom, passing through the evil twists and turns of Swamp Valley.

It was very hard to keep everyone's spirits up since everything was gray and foggy. Everything was made of mud, mud, and more **mud**!

Here and there along the river we saw sputtering mounds of earth that spewed the stinkiest smell we'd ever smelled! It smelled like everyone on the ship had bad gas. With each blast, Captain Hook cried, "Hold on to your hooks, everyone! Get a whiff of that!"

A gloomy little cloud hovered silently in the air above. It had a smell that I couldn't describe, but it seemed to contain sadness, discomfort, and regret!

THE KINGDOM OF SWAMP VALLEY

1. Fortress of the Grumbling Spearthrowers
2. Moaning Marshland
3. Mumbling Pond
4. Longface Swamp
5. Cliff of the Archers of Aggression
6. Weepy House
7. Foul Mood Forest
8. Boiling Mud Puddle
9. River of Boredom
10. Dark Castle

At least the Wicked Witch of the West had made us immune. What a mousetastic relief!

Merlin's paint job had worked perfectly, too. The inhabitants of **Swamp Valley** along the riverbank didn't give us a second glace! They just went on their way, their faces as long as ever. What luck!

The Wicked Witch suddenly sniffed at the air. "I sense the smell of sorcery — and I would know!" she cackled. "It seems as though the Great Grayness is coming from over there . . ."

She pointed at a CASTLE looming in the distance.

"Let me look," Captain Hook said, pointing his spyglass toward the castle. "Shiver me timbers! What a horrifying place!"

He passed around the SPYGLASS and we all looked, too. Yikes! The castle was a

MONSTROUS STRUCTURE MADE OF MUD!

Muddy gargoyles spouted high jets of mud, muddy spires reached for the sky, and an enormouse front gate resembling a mouth full of fangs was completely made of mud, too!

HOW FUR-RAISING!

Winglet gripped her bow and arrows. "So that's who's threatening the peace of the empire," she said, trembling with indignation. "We're going down there and putting a stop to this **cruelty**. It seems like the river will take us right to the castle. Is that right, Captain?"

Hook nodded. "Yes, but if we continue to sail this slowly, we'll arrive in a century or two!"

Just then we saw a group of ducklings appear on the water! They were as fluffy as cotton balls and looked around with big, expressive eyes!

What cute little fuzzballs!

As soon as she saw them, Winglet softened like cheese in the sun. "What darlings!" she cried, stretching out a hand to pet them.

It was so sweet!

Meanwhile, Dawn was giving the ducklings a hostile look. Narek didn't look happy, either!

"Don't lean too far over the ship, Winglet," Lorian warned. "We don't know what could be lurking in these **DANGEROUS** waters!"

Then he turned to me and lowered his voice. "She's always had a weakness for baby animals. Once, when we were little, she insisted that we bring a nest of abandoned eggs to Crystal Castle. When they hatched, they turned out to be *snakes*!"

Winglet rolled her eyes. "They were baby cobras, to be exact! But, Lorian, what harm could these sweet, defenseless little creatures possibly —"

Galloping gorgonzola! The sweet ducklings turned out to have enormouse sharp teeth!

They could have gobbled Winglet's hand right up if she hadn't snatched it back!

Quick as a flash, the ducklings attacked the ship and started to chomp at the wood with their **SHARP** teeth!

They were more voracious than a school of barracudas, and faster than a cat chasing a rat! As they gnawed at the ship, wood shavings rained down into the water!

"They're going to **devour** my ship!" Hook howled, grasping the ship's wheel like he thought he could protect the ship just by holding on to it!

But it was useless: The ducklings had created a hole in the hull. We were quickly taking on

water! Apparently, the ship was only the appetizer for these ducklings. We were the main course — rats!

"Farewell, my friends," said the Wicked Witch of the West. "It was nice knowing you!"

We were about to sink, when we heard a sudden ticking in the air.

TICK TOCK!! TICK TOCK!! TICK TOCK!! TICK TOCK!! TICK TOCK!! TICK TOCK!! TICK TOCK!!

Hook grew as pale as ricotta. "Oh no! I can't believe it! That terrible sound again! He's here!"

"Who?" I asked, my fur standing on end.

Hook cried, "**THE CROCODILE!**"

HOOK IS MINE . . . AND I'M GOING TO EAT HIM!

For the love of cheese!

A gigantic **CROCODILE** was swimming quickly toward the terrifying ducklings, baring his teeth!

The ducklings launched themselves at him, but as soon as they saw his smile and his **three hundred teeth** . . .

Quack!

Quack! Quack! Quack!

The dangerous ducklings swam away as fast as they could go, flapping their wings with **fright**!

We couldn't believe our eyes. The crocodile had scared them off and saved us! He was our hero!

Just then the ferocious reptile laid his famished, meat-hungry **EYES** on Captain Hook. Hook began to run around the ship in a panic, but the crocodile didn't lose sight of him for a second!

"Get me out of here!" Hook screeched. He scrambled up the mainmast but slipped. At the last moment, he grabbed one of the ship's ropes.

He wasn't fast enough. The crocodile jumped out of the water at lightning speed and snapped clear through Hook's pants with his jaws!

"OW!" Hook cried.

The Wicked Witch, however, burst into laughter!

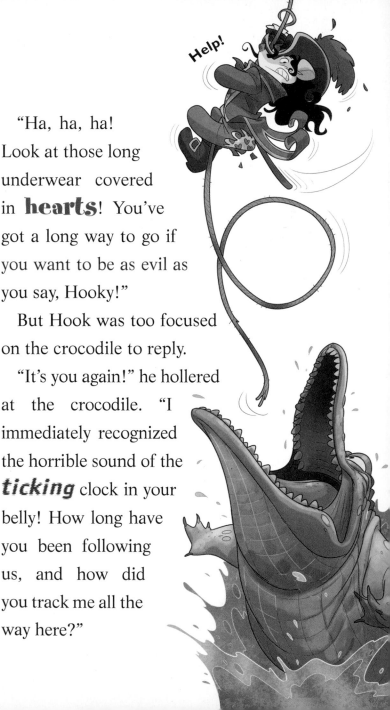

"Ha, ha, ha! Look at those long underwear covered in **hearts**! You've got a long way to go if you want to be as evil as you say, Hooky!"

But Hook was too focused on the crocodile to reply.

"It's you again!" he hollered at the crocodile. "I immediately recognized the horrible sound of the *ticking* clock in your belly! How long have you been following us, and how did you track me all the way here?"

"**GRRRR!**" the crocodile replied.

Luckily, Lorian understood the language of dragons, so he also knew something about how crocodiles communicated. He tried to interpret the **growling**.

"Dear captain," Lorian called up to Hook, "I think that this lively reptile came here because he wants to be the one to take a bite out of you!"

The crocodile nodded, almost affectionately.

"**GRRR, GRRRR, GRRRR!**"

He began to swim in circles around the ship.

Lorian continued. "Believe it or not, Captain, you're his favorite prey!"

"Lucky me," Hook said, rolling his eyes.

"And it looks like he wants to join us on our journey," the Wicked Witch noted.

"Sure, until the adventure is over," said Hook. "Then he'll gobble me up!"

"Oh, he seems awfully cute," Winglet

murmured. "Look, he's also covered in mud so that he could slip into Swamp Valley without being noticed. What a smart croc!"

"Here we go again," Lorian said with a sigh.

Winglet wasn't bothered. "I have a feeling that this **CROCODILE** will keep us company during our mission. I think he could help us, just like he did when those crazy ducklings attacked us."

The Wicked Witch of the West said, "I hate to

interrupt, but aren't you all forgetting something? The ship is **flooding**!"

Squeak! She was right!

With all the skill of a pirate in the middle of a raging storm, Captain Hook patched the leak in the twitch of a whisker. Then he also patched his trousers, using his hook as a needle! I had to admit, he was a very resourceful pirate.

The crocodile just kept swimming around us, giving his old rival a hungry look now and then. He was ready to defend his prey. I just hoped he wasn't getting any ideas about gobbling up a mousely morsel in the meantime!

THE GRAY WATCH

We continued to sail down the river, but the journey was so slow that it felt like it might never end!

The crocodile swimming alongside us had my tail in a twist. Instead of getting closer, our destination appeared to be getting farther and farther away. The castle wavered in the mist of the Great Grayness like a mirage. It was starting to feel impawssible that we could finish this mission.

"We'll never get there! Never!" the Wicked Witch of the West complained.

Winglet tried to console her. "We can't give up now. We have to stay positive! Where's your grit? Have you forgotten that you're the scariest character from *The Wonderful Wizard of Oz*?"

"Oh, I know." The witch sighed. "But darkness and despair are part of my nature, too! I'm the Witch of the West, where the sun sets. My dearly departed sister, the Witch of the East, was all sunshine and happiness because she lives where the sun rises! Oh, suddenly I miss her so much."

Holey cheese, I actually felt sorry for her! After all, I'm a very sensitive mouse. Her **gloominess** made me feel gloomy, too!

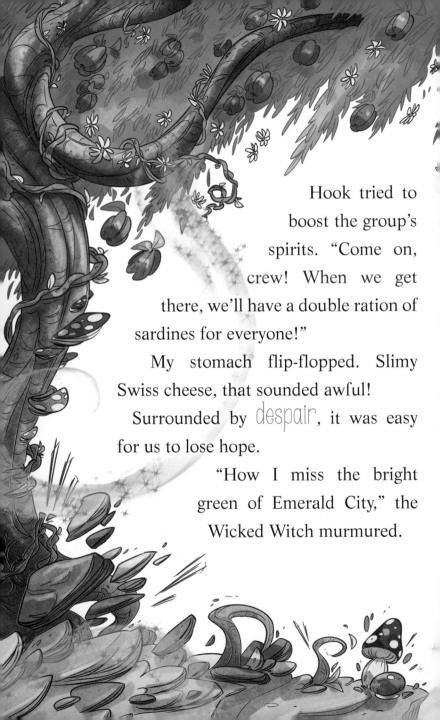

Hook tried to boost the group's spirits. "Come on, crew! When we get there, we'll have a double ration of sardines for everyone!"

My stomach flip-flopped. Slimy Swiss cheese, that sounded awful!

Surrounded by despair, it was easy for us to lose hope.

"How I miss the bright green of Emerald City," the Wicked Witch murmured.

Feeling low, I peered around at the damp ground of the riverbank. It was all gray, gray, gray . . . yellow . . . red . . . blue . . . pink . . . green . . . purple . . .

What? How? Where had those colors come from?! Had I ever seen flowers like that before? Had I just imagined them?

POOF! POOF! POOF!

Thundering cattails! I could even smell them. They had to be real. I really had seen them! In the middle of all that gray, there were bushes full of beautiful, colorful, fragrant flowers!

I pointed a paw. "Look!"

POOF!   POOF!

In another spot along the bank, a tree bursting with leaves and fruit exploded from the ground!

"That's incredible!" Winglet cried, her eyes bright. "Look over there . . . and there . . . and there!"

Just when we had been about to give in to sadness, this sight warmed our hearts. Everywhere we looked, plants, branches, and flowers were popping up! How could this be?

"PUT IT OUT!" a voice shouted through a megaphone. A cart arrived on the shore with sirens blaring. Holey cheese, what an earsplitting racket!

The side of the cart read:

THE GRAY WATCH.

"Dangerous **MULTICOLORED** bud sighting! Proceed with the moldy flood!" a Gray One shouted through the megaphone.

Three Gray Ones dressed in gray uniforms and firefighters' helmets took a huge hose and pointed it toward the plants. A **POWERFUL** spray hit the fruits and flowers. In the twitch of a whisker, they **FADED**!

The Gray Watch worked quickly, and nature's beauty disappeared before our very eyes! All those beautiful colors, gone in seconds. It was as if they had put out a fire of joy!

The watchman with the megaphone declared, "**Mission accomplished!** We have to move quickly; there has been another dangerous bud sighting near Mumbling Pond. Let's go!"

They rushed away, as quick as they'd come, leaving a *carpet* of gray despair behind them.

"Oh no," the Wicked Witch of the West murmured.

"Oh yes!" said Winglet.

We all looked at her confused. How could she be happy at a time like this?

"Nature is being suffocated," Winglet said. "That is **terrible**, and we have to find a way to stop it. But, it's great that we were even able to find these beautiful flowers. It means there is still **hope**!"

"That's true. Well said, noble Empress!" Captain Hook raised his hook in approval.

Winglet turned to him with a **smile**. "Even though the Gray Watch put all of the color out, more will pop up soon. Otherwise, why would they bother **creating** a force to put them out?"

My heart melted like cheese in the sun.

The **FLOWERS** that had popped up in the middle of all that grayness had reminded us that we had something to **protect**, not just an enemy to fight. Cheese and crackers, it was nice to feel hopeful again!

A HALF WORD
TOO MUCH

Encouraged and full of energy, we continued our voyage toward the Dark Castle. Even the Wicked Witch of the West was back in a good mood.

"I feel much better!" the witch said cheerfully. "Those emerald-green leaves were WOND—" ♡

She was in the middle of speaking when . . .

POOF!

Her nose disappeared!

"Hey, where did it go?" she cried, looking down at the end of her snout.

Luckily, because she hadn't finished saying the word before, her **nose** reappeared!

Winglet sighed. "I think we've just discovered one of

the words from the Parchment of Positivity," she said. "If you had finished saying that word, you would have disappeared and transformed into a Shapeless One!"

Crusty cat litter, what a close call!

Lorian frowned. "We must be more careful."

"How can we?" I asked. "To us, it's second nature to speak this way! I can't help that I am a positive mouse."

Lorain thought for a moment. "When we want to use a positive word, to be safe, we should use *SYNONYMS*, or **WORD PLAY**!"

Hook snapped his fingers. "Right! So, Witch, you should have said, 'Those emerald-green leaves *weren't revolting*!'"

"Bravo!" said Lorian.

"Grrr!" the crocodile roared. He seemed to like his favorite prey's sense of humor.

The Wicked Witch **TEASED** the pirate. "Listen

here, sardine-eater: Your hook isn't so useless after all. It could open boxes!"

"That didn't make me laugh, and it's off the subject," Hook muttered.

But I thought it was very, very funny! I can't help it, I'm a mouse with a great sense of humor.

I said, "Madam witch, you say you have a soul full of despair, but your jokes make me so **cheer** —" ♡

POOF!

I stopped just in time! My **tail** had disappeared!

"Oops!" I said. "I meant to say that your jokes are full of hum —" ♡

POOF! POOF!

Help!

Rancid ricotta!
Now my **ears** had
vanished, too!
That was the moment
that I started to **PANIC**!

My brain turned to mush, and I began to babble. "Oops! No! I meant to say that your jokes are funny, unique, truly enchant —" ♥

POOF!   POOF!   POOF!

I stopped just in time, but my whiskers and my **nose** had also disappeared!

"Oops! No! I wanted to say that your jokes are a real gas, a —"

Stop!" Winglet said.

I clapped a paw over my snout . . .

. . . and a moment later, my tail, ears, nose, and whiskers reappeared! Rat-munching rattlesnakes, that was

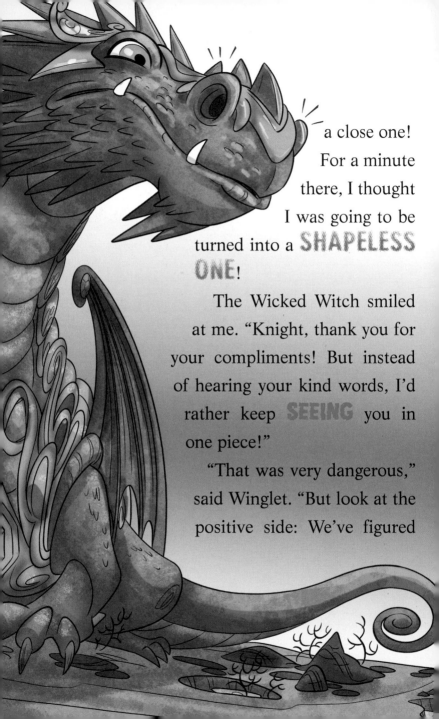

a close one! For a minute there, I thought I was going to be turned into a SHAPELESS ONE!

The Wicked Witch smiled at me. "Knight, thank you for your compliments! But instead of hearing your kind words, I'd rather keep SEEING you in one piece!"

"That was very dangerous," said Winglet. "But look at the positive side: We've figured out **FOUR** of the nine forbidden words on the Parchment of Positivity!"

Rats and cats, she was right! I had risked my tail, but at least we had taken a step forward!

We were all sharing satisfied smiles when Dawn, Narek, and the crocodile started acting **NERVOUS**. Had they sensed something?

Winglet stroked the tiger's fur. "Dawn, what's bothering you?" She paused. "I don't know why, but I feel a bit like we're being watched . . ."

At that moment, we noticed two enormouse round eyes peeking out at us from the branches of a willow tree on the riverbank. *Squeak!*

"INTRUDERS! INTRUDERS!"

shouted a creature, jumping out of the shadows.

Oh, for the love of cheese!

It was a giant, scaly gray CHAMELEON!

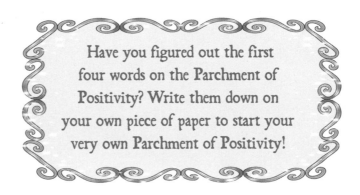

Have you figured out the first four words on the Parchment of Positivity? Write them down on your own piece of paper to start your very own Parchment of Positivity!

The Gray Chameleon

The slimy creature hollered, "Alert! Alert! Alert!"

Chattering cheddar, now we would surely be caught!

The chameleon was shouting itself hoarse when it noticed the crocodile on the surface of the water. A piece of the crusty **mud** that covered the croc had come loose, revealing its scaly green skin!

The chameleon suddenly changed its tune. "What a beautiful color! I can't resist!" Without hesitating, it launched itself right onto the **CROCODILE'S** back!

Hook commented, "That might not have been a good idea, little lizard. I suggest you start **swimming**!"

The chameleon didn't realize its mistake until the crocodile gnashed its sharp TEETH!

"Help!" the little creature wailed, swimming quickly toward the ship. The crocodile was right on its tail!

Lorian didn't hesitate. He jumped into the disgusting water and grabbed the chameleon, holding it out of reach of the crocodile. Lorian was taking a big risk! He was bold and fearless, like a true KNIGHT.

In the end, he managed to tame the crocodile and keep the chameleon safe. Together, we all helped pull him and the chameleon both back onto the ship.

"Who are you? What do you want with us?" Winglet asked the chameleon, her eyes flashing.

The reptile spluttered, "I — I — I am a gray chameleon, and I work as a l-l-lookout for the Invisible Army!"

"A gray chameleon?" I asked.

"Yes!" he said. "I am a very **RARE** type of thousand-year-old chameleon. I lived here when the Kingdom of Swamp Valley was still the Kingdom of Blossom Valley. I adored the different **COLORS** of nature and loved stepping onto all the different colors to try to discover new shades!" He frowned. "But after Hordus's curse, everything turned gray . . . including me! I became a **GRAY CHAMELEON**. Since then, I've always felt sad. But when I saw the green crocodile, I felt my old love for color awaken! I couldn't resist."

A tear rolled down his face. "I miss nature so much!"

"Oh, talking lizard, what a sad story!" Hook murmured. That old pirate was as tender as string cheese. "That hurts my poor hea —" ♡

Just then his **HOOK** disappeared! Thankfully, he had stopped himself in time, and — POOF!

The hook reappeared.

Captain Hook laughed loudly. "I lost my hook for a moment, but we've found the FIFTH word from the Parchment of Positivity!"

The Gray Chameleon was still lost in his own memories. "Once I tried to jump on one of those multicolored flowers that

What is the fifth word on the Parchment of Positivity? Write it down on your own Parchment of Positivity.

GAME
Gray Chameleon conceals himself using color. You'll find him here eight times if you look carefully!

pops up in the swamp. I just wanted to turn myself blue, yellow, even brown. Anything but gray! But it's forbidden. The Gray Ones have forced me to give up all **COLORS**! They spare me only because I'm the perfect lookout. I can conceal myself anywhere!"

The chameleon sighed. "I should signal to the Gray Ones to let them know you're here, but that brave knight risked his life to save me from the crocodile." He pointed to Lorian. "I must repay him!"

"Any help would be most welcome," Winglet said kindly. "We've been sailing toward the **DARK CASTLE** to fight the source of the Great Grayness, but it always seems to escape us. We can never reach it!"

Gray Chameleon nodded. "You'll never reach it by sailing along the river. That's another one of Hordus's **SPELLS**: No one can enter

Argh!

the castle except its master!"

"Crusty cheese curds!" I murmured. "There's no escape. Now we'll never bring HARMON —" ♡

Rats, my paw was disappearing! Luckily, I had stopped myself from speaking in time. I trembled like melty mozzarella, but I had discovered the **SIXTH** word on the Parchment of Positivity!

Gray Chameleon smiled. "Knight, don't worry! I know the secret to reaching the Dark Castle. You can get there only through the precious Infinite Seed. It's the seed from which the Kingdom of Blossom Valley grew!"

What is the sixth word on the Parchment of Positivity? Write it down on your Parchment of Positivity!

We were all **silent** for a moment, thinking hard.

"Where can we find it?" Winglet asked.

"On Hazy Mountain, the highest peak in the kingdom," Gray Chameleon revealed. "I cannot say more than that!"

"That's more than enough," Winglet said.

Gray Chameleon frowned. "You must be very **careful** around the seed's master, the Sovereign of Sadness and the Black Arts. He darkens the darkness, grays the grayness, depresses the depressed, and changes good to evil. It's **impossible** to escape his power!"

Yikes, my whiskers were already trembling with fear!

Before saying good-bye, Winglet gave Gray Chameleon a small gift — one of the cobalt-blue **NUTS** that we had gotten at the Fantasy Fair! She had kept it in her pocket, and Merlin's painting spell hadn't turned it gray.

"Take this and keep it hidden!" the empress said. "This can be our secret. It will give you courage and remind you of the colors of the

while you wait for its splendor to return!"

Gray Chameleon held the nut tightly. A cobalt-blue tinge appeared on his toes as a small TEAR fell from his eye.

"Did you say that the colors will return?" he asked quietly.

"I didn't just say it," Winglet declared. "I PROMISED!"

To the Dizzying Hazy Mountain

We continued our journey, this time toward Hazy Mountain. It stood out against the sky as gray, imposing, gloomy, and very, very tall!

What rotten luck! It seems like every adventure I've had has involved climbing a dizzyingly tall, rocky peak! But I got strength from the thought that the precious seed was up there and would allow us to complete our mission.

We went around a small bend in the river, and then the moment we feared had arrived. We had to abandon ship and set our paws on the muddy, stinky ground!

"Stay **STRONG**, crew!" Hook said.

Then he tossed a rotten wooden plank toward the riverbank, creating a bridge between the ship and the land.

The Wicked Witch was the last one to cross, but I could see that she was hesitating. She was holding her umbrella between herself and the river, and she looked tremendmousely terrified! It was as if she was afraid of the **water**!

Lorian gallantly offered her a hand. "Don't be afraid. The bridge is solid," he said, right before the plank let out a loud **CRAAAACK!**

Hook chuckled. "Ha, ha, ha! My dear witch,

Oh no, water!

Ha, ha, ha!

you've got a long way to go before you'll be a real villain!"

"Look who's talking, fish bait!" the witch said. "It's not my fault that I was created this way in *The Wonderful Wizard of Oz*. Water is my greatest enemy. Just one splash, and I'll **MELT** like butter!"

So that's why the witch carried an **UMBRELLA**

everywhere! And that's why she had objected when Hook suggested traveling by river!

In the end, the Wicked Witch made it across the plank, and we set off toward Hazy Mountain.

"Everyone has **fears**, don't worry about it," I told her, trying to be a gentlemouse.

Looking at me with admiration, Winglet said, "But you, my friend, have no fear. That's why you're the Guardian of the Realm!"

"Me?" I said. I could hardly believe my ears! "I'm the biggest scaredy-mouse of us all!"

We trudged across wet, muddy ground. "Ugh, how awful!" Winglet said.

Lorian smiled. "When we were kids, you loved playing in the mud. I remember that you'd wait for rain, and then run out into the muddy woods. You always got me dirty, too! Your mother didn't know what to do with you. You'd come back covered in **mud** from head to toe!"

Winglet hid her smile behind her curls. "Mother," she whispered. "Even now I'm sure she doesn't know what to do with me. At least when I was little, I only played in the mud. Now I get myself in much bigger trouble!"

"Don't say that," I squeaked, trying to cheer her up. "You're on a quest to save the empire! Blossom is proud of you!"

Lorian agreed. "Yes, even when you were a little girl, she was happy that you were so independent, lively, with such a big imaginat —" ♡

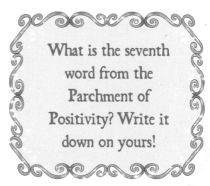

What is the seventh word from the Parchment of Positivity? Write it down on yours!

Thundering cattails! Lorian's **aRm** had disappeared!

My arm!

Luckily, he stopped speaking just in time. His arm reappeared magically!

Plus, we'd figured out the **SeVeNtH** word from the Parchment of Positivity!

Winglet let out a sigh of relief and put an arm around the dragon tamer. "Lorian, be careful! If we lost you, I . . ." The empress paused before speaking again. "You followed me on this risky **MISSION**, and if it fails, so does the empire. Maybe I should have listened to my mother and waited for the council. But if the enemy had attacked us because I waited too long to act, it would have been my **RESPONSIBILITY**, too. Either way, the weight is on me!"

Poor Empress! Her job was harder than a lump of old Parmesan.

"Winglet," Lorian said, taking her hands, "you regained the crown and reunited an empire that was thought lost. I'm convinced that your COURAGE shines like a star in the midst of the Grayness. We are all on your side."

What a moving speech!

"Yes, don't be sad," the Wicked Witch of the West added. "As my sister, the Witch of the East, says: 'Life is bitter, but with a bit of **sweetn**—'" ♡

POOF!

"Oh! One of my feet disappeared!" the witch cried.

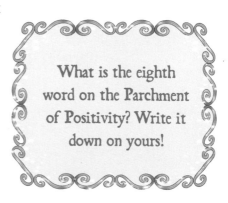

What is the eighth word on the Parchment of Positivity? Write it down on yours!

I clapped my paws. "We just figured out the **eighth** word from the Parchment of

Positivity! Now we're only missing one, and then we'll know all the words we can't say in Swamp Valley!"

We forged ahead, but before long, we heard a rustling.

Then a shout made my fur stand on end. "**Let loose!**"

All of a sudden, a handful of Invisibles must have leaped out from behind a bush, aiming a catapult at us. We were bombarded by muddy, festering **mud bubbles**! Rats!

STRESS
BUBBLES

Rat-munching rattlesnakes, how gross!

The Invisibles must have found us while we were talking, sharing the elements of friendship that were forbidden in Swamp Valley!

Now there were so many mud bubbles, and they were coming from everywhere!

"KEEP AT IT, MY REVOLTING NOTHINGS!"

the general thundered. I recognized him immediately: It was Cruelardo Glowerface, the general of the Invisible Army!

I was shaking in my fur at the sight of him!

Little by little, as the mud bubbles hit us, we felt more tired and worn out.

"Oh, oh, ohhhh," Hook moaned. "I feel as

broken down as an ancient shipwreck!"

"Me too! I feel like falling over," the Wicked Witch groaned.

"I'm so **sad**," said Winglet.

"And so bitter," said Lorian.

My whiskers wobbled with the stress and sadness of it all! Even Narek, Dawn, and the crocodile were shrouded in despair.

"Ha, ha!" Cruelardo cackled. "The Stress Bubbles have taken effect on you. It looks like you aren't really part of Swamp Valley!"

Cheese niblets, could things get any **WOrse**?

The devious Cruelardo continued. "We've been watching you for a while, imposters!"

One of his followers burst out, "I spotted you first!"

"Quiet!" the general spat. "Here **I** do the talking, **I** decide what we do, **I** — Ooh, but look

who we have here. It's the empress herself!"

And he gave Winglet an icy *GLARE*.

"Yes, it is!" Winglet confronted him, shaking off the effect of the Stress Bubbles.

"I never dreamed I'd have such a fruitful fishing trip!" Cruelardo gloated. "This will please my ruler, the Sovereign of Sadness and the Black Arts, he who darkens the darkness, grays the grayness, depresses the depressed, and turns good into evil. He will transform you into *SHAPELESS ONES*!"

"Take me and leave my companions alone," Winglet said, her eyes flashing.

"Ha, ha, ha!" Cruelardo mocked her. "Sure! Would you like me to pack a snack for their trip, too? How ridiculous!"

"Don't speak that way to the empress," I said, with a sudden burst of **COURAGE**. I couldn't stand that fontina face treating Winglet badly!

The general looked at me suspiciously. "Your snout looks familiar. Turning you into a Shapeless One is going to be a piece of cake — or, rather, cheese!"

"No!" Winglet shouted.

But it was too late: Cruelardo's henchmen began to tie us up!

"**ONWARD!**" Cruelardo shouted, urging on his soldiers. "To the Lake of Broken Dreams! My ruler will be very satisfied with my work."

"Uh, excuse me, what's the Lake of Broken Dreams?" I murmured.

The general sneered. "It's the place where the enemies of sadness become Shapeless Ones! Now you must resign yourself to your fate, mouse. It's a long walk!"

To the Hissing Secrets

I t looked like our adventure would soon come to an end. Our dreams were vanishing before our eyes. We were going to become Shapeless Ones!

I could hardly believe it. We were **prisoners**!

As we marched, the Invisibles sang:

"Onward, onward, march your feet

To the Hissing Secrets, where you admit defeat!"

Onward, prisoners!

I didn't like the sound of that one tiny bit. Just the name HISSING SECRETS made my fur stand on end!

As evening fell, we arrived at a big shack made of cement with only one tiny window. Every single piece of my fur was exhausted!

Cruelardo smiled cruelly. "The JOURNEY is long. A night in the Hissing Secrets will refresh you!" He snapped his fingers at two of the guards. "Keep watch while I rest and I polish the weapons!"

Before we knew it, we were shut in a damp,

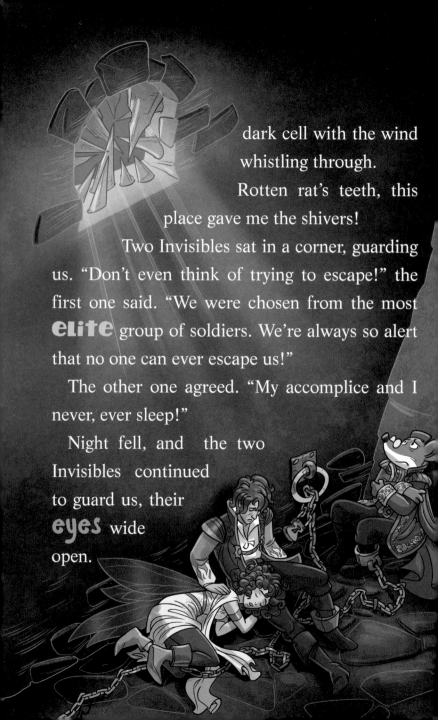

dark cell with the wind whistling through.

Rotten rat's teeth, this place gave me the shivers!

Two Invisibles sat in a corner, guarding us. "Don't even think of trying to escape!" the first one said. "We were chosen from the most **elite** group of soldiers. We're always so alert that no one can ever escape us!"

The other one agreed. "My accomplice and I never, ever sleep!"

Night fell, and the two Invisibles continued to guard us, their **eyes** wide open.

"I'm sorry," Winglet whispered to us. "I wanted to save you all, but I couldn't!"

"It's not your fault," I said. "And there's still **hope**!"

We all gathered around Winglet, so tired and worn out that we fell into a deep sleep. My final thought before falling asleep was of my friend Blossom, who was waiting for us at Crystal Castle. How worried she must be! Who knew if we would ever return to her?

In the morning, I was awakened by **sunlight** shining through the window.

I was covered with bruises from sleeping on the ground, and my tail had fallen asleep. Holey cheese, the floor of that cell was awfully uncomfortable!

"The galley on my ship was a five-star hotel compared to this," Hook grumbled.

The Wicked Witch of the West moaned. "I

challenge anyone to take a decent nap in this place."

SNore! ZZZZ   SNore! ZZZZ

SNore! ZZZZ

Rancid ricotta! The guards were snoring like hibernating bears! But how? Hadn't they said that they never slept?

This was our chance! Maybe, if we moved very, very, verrrrrry slowly, we could ESCAPE!

We tiptoed toward the door, but something wasn't right. Quiet as a rat, I turned to Lorian,

Where's Winglet?

who had turned to the Wicked Witch of the West, who had turned to Captain Hook, who had turned to the crocodile, who had turned to Dawn, who had turned to Narek, who had turned to . . .

At that very moment, my whiskers twisted with fear. **Winglet had disappeared!**

WINGLET, WHERE ARE YOU?

"**O**h no!" I cried.

"Oh no!" my friends echoed.

"Oh no!" the guards cried, waking up. "We fell asleep! Now Cruelardo will make us direct mosquito traffic at Longface Swamp as punishment!"

My heart POUNDED under my fur. I couldn't believe my eyes. My friend, the sweet, strong, unique, and brave *Rebel Empress*, was nowhere to be seen!

Maybe Cruelardo had taken her away while we were sleeping?

Just then the evil general banged open the door.

"Where is the empress?" he shouted.

Holey cheese, he hadn't been the one to take Winglet away!

Don't play games!

"Don't play games!" he roared. "Where is she hiding?"

"Um," I squeaked up. "Actually, we thought maybe you were hiding her somewhere!"

Cruelardo grew even angrier. "**WHAT?!** What kind of trick is this? Witch, did you cast a spell? Mouse, is this your fault? You'll pay for

Where is Winglet?

GENERAL
CRUELARDO
GLOWERFACE

this! I'll take you straight to the Lake of Broken Dreams, where you'll turn into Shapeless Ones!"

Oh, why did these sorts of things always happen to me?

"And you," he added, turning to the guards, "you let our most valuable PRISONER escape! You'll soon be directing mosquito traffic at Longface Swamp!"

"Aww, we knew it!" they grumbled.

The general got down to business.

Stress Bubble Force

"A segment of the Whine-Toss Tossers will go **search** for the empress: Marshall Pessimo, Captain Bitter, and Lieutenant Sadderly, commanded by Colonel Judgment. A segment of the Arrows of Aggression Force, on the other hand, will **escort** these imposters. That segment will include Colonel Uglydud, Marshall McNasty, Captain Scour, and Lieutenant Destructo. Now march, nobodies!"

Crusty creampuffs, how were we

going to *wiggle* our way out of this one?

The Invisible Army sprang into action, attaching ropes and locks to our legs and arms and dragging us toward our new, **terrifying** destination. I felt even sadder than ever!

We walked in silence for a while. Then Dawn began to make strange sounds, like **purring**!

"You miss Winglet, don't you?" I asked the white tiger quietly.

But Dawn kept sniffing the ground, as if she could sense something . . .

Suddenly, one of the Invisibles shouted, "Hey, you *pushed* me!"

"Me?" a voice rang out.

"Yes, you! Watch it! Marshall McNasty doesn't give anyone a free pass!"

"What's going on? Are you in a worse mood than usual? Are your rations more rancid than usual? I didn't do anything!"

"What are you talking about?" the other replied.

Just then McNasty's **helmet** flew off his head, falling into the mud.

"I warned you!" he cried furiously.

"Hey, it was just the wind!" the other replied.

"I'll show you!"

And in the twitch of a whisker, they launched into a **SERIOUS BRAWL**!

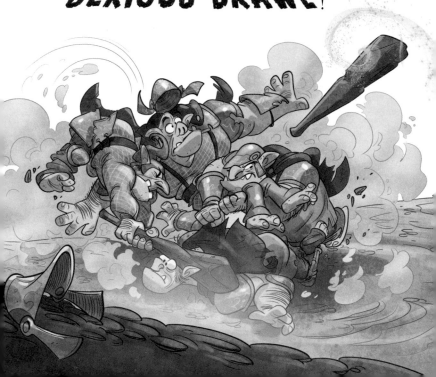

"Stop that!" Lieutenant Descructo shouted. He jumped into the fight with them! "Take that! And that!"

Cats and rats! The lieutenant was stronger than both of the others put together!

Of course, the rest of the group couldn't resist a good rumble. Before I could even squeak, there was no one left to guard us. They were all too busy fighting one another!

"Psst," Hook whispered. "They might be great warriors, but they're not very attentive guards!"

Quick as rats in a cheese factory, we leaped at the opportunity to get away. Unfortunately, we couldn't get very far, since our hands and legs were tied up!

Suddenly, we heard a metallic CLANG! Something had opened the LOCK on my hind paws. Holey cheese, I was free!

I spotted the key on the ground next to me. How had it gotten there? There was no time for questions. I grabbed it and freed my friends as quickly as I could!

Then, before our enemies got tired of fighting, **WE WERE OFF**! We scurried out of there as fast as our paws could take us!

WINGLET'S SECRET

Puff! *Pant!* After an exhausting run, we all hid behind a bush.

The Invisibles had been following us, but they had passed right by. They didn't spot us!

"Where did they go?" one asked.

"Over there!"

"No, there!"

"I said over there!"

"Don't contradict me!"

And just like that, they started another **FIGHT**!

While they were busy, we managed to sneak away again. We kept walking toward Hazy Mountain along a grueling road. Thanks to Merlin's **MAP**, we knew all of Swamp Valley's secrets!

Or at least we thought we did! Along the rough, difficult road, very strange things kept happening.

For example, while we were plodding up a hill, my paw **SLIPPED** on some gravel! I was about to roll away like a wheel of cheese when an INVISIBLE force grabbed me! Rat-munching rattlesnakes, what was it?

Plus, Lorian, who was more sad and disheartened than I'd ever seen him, suddenly found a beautiful FLOWER stuck in his hair.

What's going on?

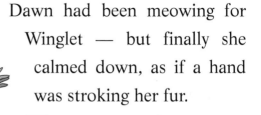

Dawn had been meowing for Winglet — but finally she calmed down, as if a hand was stroking her fur.

When we sat down on a rock to take a break, I asked my friends, "Does it seem like something STRANGE is happening around us?"

Lorian nodded. "I'm afraid to say it out loud, but I almost have the feeling that —"

I said, "It's as if —"

Even Dawn let out a kind of yelp.

We all shared a look of shock.

I finally put together all the clues. "Winglet is here with us! She didn't really disappear. She became a SHAPELESS ONE!"

Then we noticed a shape on the ground that had been traced by an invisible hand. It was a HEART! Surely this was a message from Winglet!

"Empress, you're here!" Lorian cried, a TEAR sliding down his cheek.

Hook was astounded. "You're right! The noble lady is here!"

The Wicked Witch of the West sighed. "I knew she hadn't abandoned us!"

Holey cheese, I finally understood what was happening. "Winglet, you know what the **last** word on the Parchment of Positivity is," I said. "You must have said it in order to turn into a Shapeless One. You sacrificed yourself to give us a way out!"

YOU'RE RIGHT, KNIGHT!

Winglet wrote in the dirt.

Lorian looked thoughtful. "Apparently not even the Invisibles can SEE the Shapeless

Ones once they've transformed. Winglet must have slipped out of the cell as soon as Cruelardo opened the door!"

Winglet's invisible hand wrote:

Hook said, "And she hid the key in order to free us!"

I was jumping out of my fur with the joy of knowing that the empress was right next to us!

I was so happy that I almost forgot the most **terrible** part.

Pale as ricotta, I sputtered, "Empress, you said

the ninth word on the Parchment of Positivity. That's the only one that doesn't make you stay a Shapeless One FOREVER. But how do we make you reappear among us?"

After a long pause, the reply was traced on the ground:

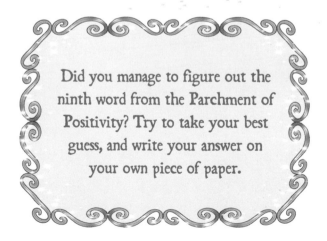

I DON'T KNOW YET.

Did you manage to figure out the ninth word from the Parchment of Positivity? Try to take your best guess, and write your answer on your own piece of paper.

THE GEM'S DISAPPEARANCE

Poor Winglet. Poor us!

Lorian and I were so distressed that we hugged each other. We might never see Winglet again, with her cornflower-blue eyes and her sunny smile. We might never hear her tinkling laughter again!

The world seemed emptier and more colorless without her voice and her face.

As if she'd read my thoughts, Winglet wrote on the ground:

I WILL ALWAYS BE BESIDE YOU, FRIENDS. NOW KEEP GOING, OR MY SACRIFICE WILL BE FOR NOTHING!

The empress was right. Even though our hearts were broken, we couldn't stop now. The Infinite Seed was still out there for us to find!

Using Merlin's map, we found a route up Hazy Mountain.

It was fabumousely difficult, but after Winglet's sacrifice, we were more determined than ever to succeed in our mission!

Now the summit of Hazy Mountain was close enough that we could see it through the mist, but when we reached the peak, we were in for a **bitter** surprise. The Infinite Seed wasn't there!

"Oh no! Look here!" said the Wicked Witch of the West, pointing to something with her umbrella. In place of the precious seed, there was a big hole!

Lorian frowned. "It seems that the seed has already been removed! That was the only way to

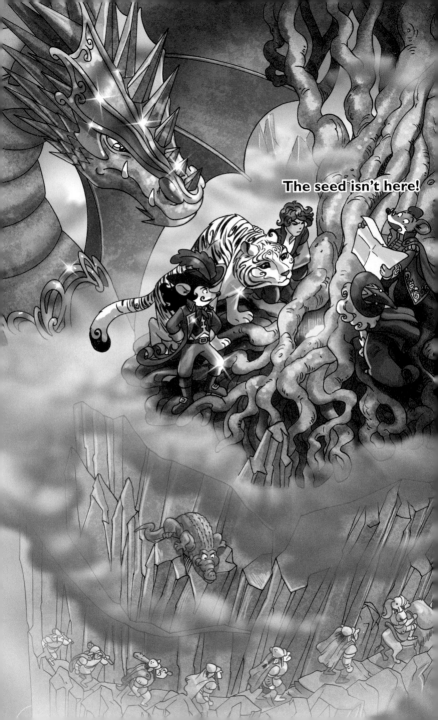

The seed isn't here!

get to Dark Castle. Now what do we do?"

Shaken to the core, I looked at the map, turning it this way and that. "Maybe we took the wrong path? Maybe we should have turned right? I don't have a very good sense of direction."

Just then an earsplitting shout echoed in the air:

"CAPTURE THE PRISONERS!"
"CAPTURE THE PRISONERS!"
"CAPTURE THE PRISONERS!"
"CAPTURE THE PRISONERS!"

It was the Invisible Army! They had found us!

There was no place to hide on that barren mountain: We would have to face them snout-to-snout!

Rats and cats, how terrifying!

I was preparing to become mouse lasagna when —

"GRRRRRRR!"

The crocodile suddenly rushed by us like a warrior, snorting and snarling!

Faced with those sharp jaws, even Cruelardo hesitated for a moment. He stepped backward and **tumbled** right into his followers. They all rolled down the slope like bowling pins!

Thanks to the crocodile, we had defeated the

Invisibles once again. Now we just needed to figure out what to do next!

That was when I peered inside the hole . . .

. . . and glimpsed an underground **tunnel** . . .

. . . and realized that it wasn't just a tunnel, but the beginning of a series of tunnels!

Suddenly, the back of the map was lit with a strange sparkling. The confusing drawing wasn't a simple decoration like we'd thought — it was a map of the tunnels!

Maybe we were supposed to explore them!

I was squeakless. The **ROOTS** of the seed were so big, deep, and wide that they had left an infinite web underneath the Kingdom of Swamp Valley!

Whiskers wobbling, I turned to Dawn and Narek. "Wait for us here with the crocodile. It's your job to make sure that Cruelardo doesn't follow us. We're going to go deeper into this mysterious world!"

THE LIGHT
IN THE TUNNEL

My dear rodent friends, you'd imagine that an underground tunnel would be as **DARK** as the inside of a cat's belly, right?

Well, that's what I thought, too, before taking this tunnel!

Fine golden DUST covered the walls, making them bright as daylight. There was more

Amazing!

light underground than aboveground!

"What a strange place," said the Wicked Witch of the West. "This tunnel sparkles in a way that reminds me of the green of Emerald City."

As we went deeper into the tunnel, we ran right into a creature dressed in a golden SUIT!

He lived in Swamp Valley but wasn't a Gray One? Cheese and crackers, that was impawssible!

As soon as the creature saw us, he gasped, "Oh no! You've found us!"

I had forgotten Merlin had disguised us so well that we really did look like GRAY ONES!

But Lorian reassured the creature. "Kind sir, we are not your enemies! We are in disguise so that we can defeat the Great Grayness. We're here on behalf of Empress Winglet."

The creature looked at us **suspiciously**, but then saw the color of Lorian's eyes. They were lively and brilliant. Those eyes couldn't possibly belong to a Gray One!

He smiled and said, "Then you are welcome here! Allow me to introduce myself. I am Gilder, and I'm one of the Underground People. Follow me, and come meet King Multicolor!"

Without another word, the creature turned and walked down a long tunnel. We followed, and before long, my fur stood on end! Holey cheese! Up ahead was a **secret city**, shining with light, hiding underground. There was no gray in sight!

Just then the king arrived, wearing a long **rainbow** cloak. Gilder presented us, and the king greeted us warmly. "The Underground People are pleased to welcome you!"

I bowed. "I never imagined that a world of **COLOR** was hiding beneath the swamp!"

King Multicolor said, "We've lived here for generations and generations. When Hordus turned the Kingdom of Blossom Valley into the Kingdom of Swamp Valley, he made his **curse** even more powerful by removing the Infinite Seed. He did that to keep Swamp Valley from turning back into Blossom Valley when the empire was reunited."

Crusty cat litter! That's why something went wrong when Winglet found the imperial crown!

It's an honor to be here!

King Multicolor continued. "Our ancestors found refuge where the **roots** of the seed once grew. The light that shines in our world is produced by the fine golden powder that covered the roots. It still covers the walls of the tunnels."

"It's like an underground **sun**!" I marveled. "And it's allowed you to live down here for generations?"

The king nodded. "Here, peace and harmony still reign, and no one has become a Gray One. We can grow flowers, fruits, and vegetables. In fact, there's so much energy that now and then **multicolored buds** pop up aboveground!"

Lorian's eyes grew wide. "Ah, so that's where they came from!"

I gazed at the world around us, astonished.

Even when all seemed lost, beauty never truly disappeared. It was just waiting to be reborn!

King Multicolor suddenly turned sad. "We've waited for a long time to return aboveground! But we know that Swamp Valley is expanding because of the GREAT GRAYNESS."

Gilder chimed in. "All of that grayness comes from the muddy Dark Castle. No one knows who really lives between those walls! They call him the Sovereign of Sadness and the Dark Arts, he who darkens the darkness, who grays the grayness, depresses the depressed, and turns good into evil — but no one has ever seen him. For centuries, we've waited for **THE ONE** who will defeat him. The legends say that one day they will come!"

"Only they can save us," the king said. "For now, come with us to the Hall of Legends and see its splendor!"

IT'S REALLY YOU!

More curious than ever, we followed His Majesty and Gilder to a shimmering hall.

Inside was filled with statues, carvings, and murals of this mysterious hero who would save them all.

In the middle of the hall, there was even an enormouse statue draped in precious stones!

King Multicolor proclaimed, "It will be a hero with a pure heart, a flowing tail, ears of —"

Wait just one whisker-licking minute! The hero was a **MOUSE**!

"Now that I can see you better . . ." the king said, peering at me, "the hero looks like — you! It must be you, mouse! I didn't recognize you, all covered in gray!"

"It's true, he's the hero!" cried Gilder.

It couldn't be me! I'm more of a 'fraidy mouse. I wanted to clear up the misunderstanding before anyone got the wrong idea, so I bowed like a **gentlemouse**. "Oh, I'm not a hero, just a simple mouse!"

King Multicolor shared a knowing look with Gilder. "The legends say that the hero will be heroic and brave, but that he will also be **MODEST!**"

It does look like me!

Captain Hook patted me on the back (luckily, not with his 𝖍𝗈𝗈𝗄!) and cried, "I did say that you're truly a special mouse!"

King Multicolor gathered his councilors, dignitaries, relatives, and friends before I could even squeak. He wanted everyone to meet me, even though I'm really a very *shy* mouse!

"Quick, quick! Let's prepare a great banquet!" he cried. "The hero has arrived!"

Rats!

They had all mistaken me for a hero who was destined to save them!

On the other paw, the banquet they prepared really was whisker-licking good. There were all kinds of delicacies, such as bowls of multicolored flower petals, cobalt-blue apples, and herb-and-lily pie.

Yum!

It seemed strange to be able to find these foods underground. The golden LIGHT left by the seed's roots was so pure and healthy that it made the colorful plants grow as if they had been kissed by the summer sun!

"I think we've earned a break," Hook declared, munching on a fruit that looked similar to a mango.

"For once, you're right, you old barnacle!" replied the Wicked Witch, biting into a purple carrot.

I had to smile. These kinds of peaceful moments were precious for our group. We hadn't realized how tired, hungry, and fed up with the Grayness we were!

Once we were refreshed, the king said, "It's time for you to go, heroes. The route to the Dark Castle goes through here and only here. But first, you must pass TWO OBSTACLES: the lair of Euridice, the Literary Mole, and the nest of Sandy, the Underground Armadillo. Only you have hope of surviving these strange creatures."

Hope of surviving?

Strange creatures?

Oh, I'm too fond of my furrrrr!

EURIDICE, THE LITERARY MOLE

Before we headed off again, the king said, "Don't worry, we'll help you!"

He introduced us to a special assistant: She looked bright and had vibrant purple hair.

"Along the way, there will be many obstacles to pass," the king explained. "Violet will help you face them in order to reach the end of your mission. Now go. We believe in you!"

We said good-bye to the king and Gilder and continued on our mission. We were going to find the **DARK WIZARD**!

Our path was truly a tangle of tunnels. They seemed to twist endlessly into the belly of the Kingdom of Swamp Valley! Suddenly, we heard a groan from deep within one of the tunnels.

Violet announced, "We've reached the library

of Euridice, the **Literary Mole**. Be careful, and whatever you do, don't contradict her!"

I stuck out my snout and could see a gigantic **mole** surrounded by hundreds — no, thousands — of books!

The mole's nose was buried in the pages of a book. She wore a pair of **glasses** with huge lenses, as thick and round as the portholes of a ship. She could probably barely see at all!

"Oof, I need to get new glasses," she grumbled, cleaning her lenses on her fur.

We cautiously stepped forward. "Excuse us, Ms. Euridice," I said. "We need to pass through your **library** in order to defeat the dark wizard!"

"Who are you?" she asked. "I can hear you, but I can't see you! It's such torture having so many **books** around and not being able to read most of them!"

I think I knew what she meant — that would be **fabumousely** hard for me, too!

The mole invited us in. "Come closer so that I can see you! Closer . . . closer . . . CLOSER!"

I was trembling in my fur! Was this mole going to do something sinister?

"Ah!" she cried, squinting at us with her tiny eyes. "Why, you are Captain Hook and the Wicked Witch of the West! This is a dream come true! I adore *Peter Pan* and *The Wonderful Wizard of Oz*. I've read them both fifty times!"

"Then we are FRIENDS and you'll let us pass?" Hook asked with a crafty smile.

"No way!" the mole snapped. "It's a dream to have you here, because I've always wanted to teach you a lesson. You should leave my heroes, Peter and Dorothy, alone! I'll squash you back into the pages of my books where you belong! And I will use you as bookmarks. Maybe that will stop you from **endangering** those young heroes!"

Violet whispered, "I think we should probably try something different. I recommend that you go after her mind. You must challenge her about what she loves most: **books**!"

Cheese niblets, that was it! But judging by her library, this mole had to have read more books than Merlin! How could we possibly beat her?

"I have an idea," Hook proposed. "Tell us the titles of your favorite **novels**, and the witch and I will summarize each of them in just five words! If we succeed, you let us pass."

The mole thought for a moment. Then her face

lit up with a grin. "I like that idea! I accept your challenge. But only because the mouse with glasses has a very kind face."

"Thank you, Ms. Euridice," I said. We were both **LITERARY** rodents, so it makes perfect sense that we got along!

The mole rubbed her paws together. "Let's begin with *Pinocchio*!"

The witch said, "Watch out when he lies!"

"Hee, hee, hee!" the mole said with a happy

giggle. "That's not bad. Now, *Treasure Island*!"

Captain Hook scratched his head, then said, "I've got it: They all want the treasure!"

The mole shrugged.

Squeak!

227

That wasn't a good sign.

Then she got so close to the captain that her nose was touching him. "That one wasn't that good!" she said sternly. "Plus, you need to comb your hair, pirate."

After a moment, the mole said, "I'll give you another one: *Around the World in Eighty Days.*"

Hook, sweating with **stress**, said, "Hope I live to return!"

"Hoo, hoo, hoo!" the mole said. Whew!

"Hee, hee, hee!" she went on. This was a really good sign!

"All right, all right, you've convinced me," Euridice said at last. "I'll let you pass. But first, a **promise**! You must behave better with my dear Peter and Dorothy. Do you understand?"

"Um, we'll try!" said Hook.

Then we all cried out, "Thank you very much, Euridice!"

Captain Hook and the Wicked Witch of the West had defeated the MOLE!

At last, we could leave that lair!

Violet grinned in excitement. "We've passed the first obstacle!" she said. "You were wonderful. Now we just need to FACE Sandy, the Underground Armadillo."

Just?
I was tying my tail in
knots thinking about that part!

Sandy, the Underground Armadillo

After convincing the mole to let us pass, we continued through the tangle of tunnels. We walked up, up, up, and then down, down, down, but there was no trace of the armadillo!

Captain Hook whispered hopefully, "Maybe the Armored One went away?"

Violet shook her head. "Don't call it the Armored One! Armadillos hold their armor very dear. Creatures like Sandy have **armor plates** that look like an elegant suit of armor, and they are very vain!"

Just then out of the corner of my eye I glimpsed a shape among the underground tunnels. I turned but didn't see a thing! After a few steps, I thought I saw another shape. But again, nothing! Rats.

Perhaps I was just seeing things. Perhaps the

armadillo really had gone on vacation. Perhaps, perhaps, perhaps . . .

RUMMMMMBLE!

Suddenly, an enormouse armadillo, all rolled up, tumbled out from a tunnel and cut off our path. It was enormouse and very fast!

"Run, run, before I catch you!" the menacing creature said.

We began to run as fast as our paws would take us! But before long, we were exhausted!

We found ourselves in a dead-end tunnel with no way to escape . . .

Holey cheese, the armadillo's gigantic head appeared right in front of us. It was opening its mouth to

GAME

Help Geronimo
and his friends find
their way out!

FINISH

The game solutions are on page 283.

gobble us up! Just then Violet said, "Over there! Look, it's a secret tunnel!"

We headed in that direction like rats with cats on our tails, and the armadillo missed us by a whisker. When we turned, we saw that the armadillo had gotten itself stuck!

"HELP ME!" she begged. "I can't get out of my armor!"

Lorian ran up to the armadillo. He looked around and saw that Sandy really was stuck, so he helped unjam plate after plate of its armor!

The armadillo sighed and smiled. "Thank you, Knight! I am in your debt. Ask me for anything, and I will do it!"

"Actually, there is something we would like to ask

you," Captain Hook and the Wicked Witch of the West said together.

Lorian added, "Sandy, take us to the **Dark Castle**!"

The armadillo nodded solemnly. "Very well! An armadillo's promise is an armadillo's promise. Jump on my back!"

Violet waved at us. "You can do it! Our *hopes* are all on you. Go!"

My whiskers trembled, but I managed to say, "Farewell, Violet. Thank you for being our guide!"

Then I climbed up onto the armadillo and tried to grip her armor as well as I could.

Squeak! She took off like a **flash**!

It wasn't easy to hold on to the armor with my paws. It was so slippery!

Sandy started to dig through one tunnel after another, moving toward the Dark Castle with Lorian helping to navigate.

"You're a great animal **tamer**!" I whispered to Lorian.

"Thank you, Knight," Lorian said with a smile. "Who knows what Winglet would say? Neither one of us would have thought that I'd tame not only dragons, but also armadillos!"

You're a great animal tamer!

At that moment, writing appeared on the ground ahead of us.

**GOOD JOB, LORIAN.
I'M PROUD OF YOU!**

Winglet was always with us, even though she was invisible. She gave us the strength and courage to push onward!

IN HORDUS'S LAIR

Sandy dug and dug until she found a *door*. It was covered in mud, stones, and soil. What was hiding on the other side? Just thinking about it made me shake in my fur!

I peered at my friends, trying to find some extra courage in their faces. We were about to enter the horrible, mysterious **Dark Castle**!

"Who knew it would be so muddy?" cried Captain Hook.

"Who knew it would be so stinky?" said the Wicked Witch of the West.

"Hold your snout!" I suggested.

But when we opened the door . . .

Whaaat?

. . . instead of holding our noses, we had to cover our eyes!

We were nearly blinded by the sparkling of topazes, rubies, diamonds, sapphires, emeralds, opals, and more! We entered a fabumouse room filled with hundreds — no, thousands — no, an infinite number of precious stones!

Golden statues spurted melted gold into golden basins, golden cornucopias overflowed with golden fruit, and gold-framed mirrors reflected other gold-framed mirrors. Wow!

The Wicked Witch of the West whispered, "I like gold, but the decor seems a bit over the top."

Holey cheese! From the outside, Dark Castle looked like a castle made of **mud**, but the inside was more luxurious than any castle I'd ever seen before!

A spectacularly dressed gentleman was dancing in the middle of the room, admiring his own reflection. Everything he wore sparkled so much that he could see himself in his shoes!

He stroked his flowing blond hair and showed off a row of dazzling teeth.

"Oh, how beautiful I am, oh, how attractive, oh, how charming, oh, how irresistible and perfect!" He sighed.

Hook scoffed, trying not to make too much noise. "Blasted buccaneers! Is this peacock the VILLAIN we must defeat?"

"We'll surely triumph!" said the witch. "Ooh, I can already smell the terror we'll wreak on the Land of Books, Hooky!"

Even I was a bit surprised! I imagined that the Sovereign of Sadness and the Black Arts, he who darkens the darkness, grays the gray, depresses the depressed, and turns good into evil would be much . . . **SCARIER**!

Lorian narrowed his eyes. "Let's not be **fooled** by his appearance. If he controls the Great Grayness, he must be much more **TERRIFYING** than he seems!"

While admiring his reflection, the king noticed something strange and let out a horrified shout. "What's this **SPOT** on my teeth? How can this be? Nothing and no one can overshadow the magnificence of the one and only, great, legendary, handsome **HORDUS**!"

Wait just one whisker-licking minute! This was Hordus, the wizard who had transformed the Kingdom of Blossom Valley into the Kingdom of Swamp Valley?

Hordus, who everyone thought had **disappeared**?

Hordus, who had transformed the inhabitants of the Kingdom of Blossom Valley into Invisibles?

Hordus was the architect of the Great Grayness?

And Hordus was still **alive**?

In a rage, he swirled his velvet

cloak and strode toward a **cauldron** that hung from one of the castle's spires.

A powerful fire burned within. It seemed to be fed by the clouds of GRAYNESS that floated outside! The flames sucked them in and became wilder as they flickered. The wizard let himself be surrounded by the warmth of the flames and suddenly he was even more young and beautiful!

"Much better," he said. "Everything has to be perfect. I must increase the Great Grayness. The greater the sadness of my people, the bigger the flames, and the greater my wealth, my power, and my beauty! *HA, HA, HA, HA, HA, H.*

He left the room in the twitch of a whisker.

Cheese niblets! That devious wizard and his palace needed everyone in Swamp Valley to stay miserable!

"Quick, let's follow him," Lorian whispered.

The Seed of Destruction

We snuck into Hordus's lair and followed him, quiet as mice. We needed to figure out what he was plotting.

There was no telling what that cheddarhead had in mind!

Hordus walked into a room that was more glamorous than the first. There was even a giant throne!

"He lives in a **FORTRESS** made of treasure," Hook whispered, flabbergasted by all the gold.

Suddenly, I noticed a big flower bud, as black as ink, shimmering in front of the throne. It pulsed as if it had a beating heart. I had a bad feeling about that thing!

What could it be?

Hordus caressed the flower bud it as if it were a pet monster.

"Great and powerful seed,
my dark masterpiece of greed!
Long ago you gave color and life,
Now the Infinite Seed is a source of strife!"

As my friends and I watched this scene from our hiding place, we couldn't believe our eyes!

I murmured, "Are you all thinking what I'm thinking?"

Lorian nodded. "That's the Infinite Seed. Hordus uprooted it and turned its magic **dark**!"

Hook clapped his good hand over his mouth. "Walloping whalebones, now what do we do?"

"Let's see what happens," the Wicked Witch of the West whispered.

Just then the dark wizard raised his hands . . . and *LIGHTNING* flashed!

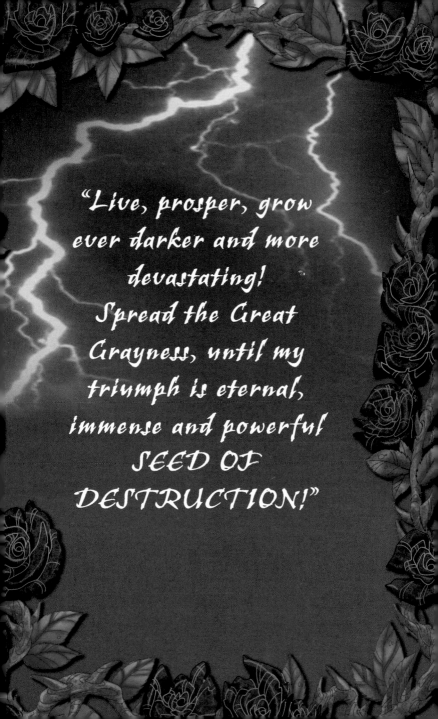

"Live, prosper, grow ever darker and more devastating! Spread the Great Grayness, until my triumph is eternal, immense and powerful SEED OF DESTRUCTION!"

At these words, the seed spun in the air, pulsing with an even **DARKER** energy. That darkness spread through the room and beyond, into the gray sky of Swamp Valley.

Rat-munching rattlesnakes!

This was a truly **EVIL** plan! Through the seed, Hordus had produced the Great Grayness, and then absorbed it.

That's how he became more and more beautiful and powerful, while everything around him overflowed with the Great Grayness!

"We must **STOP** him at any cost!" Captain Hook hissed. "I know I am a bad guy, but this villain is too terribly **EVIL**!"

"He wants to destroy the empire for his own vanity," the Wicked Witch of the West sneered. "Even when I ruled, I didn't stoop to that level of villainy!"

"**WHO IS THERE?**" Hordus suddenly thundered.

Crusty cat litter, he had discovered us!

We were so quiet, we thought there was no way he could have heard us!

We didn't have much time to devise a plan. We

all agreed with just a look. It's incredible how quickly you can make a decision when you have a Dark Wizard on your tail!

I was so nervous, I just wanted to run back in the opposite direction.

Winglet must have sensed my fear because suddenly, a message appeared on the ground:

YOU CAN DO THIS! YOU MUST STOP HIM!

Comforted by the empress's presence, I squeaked up. "Our only hope of stopping the **GREAT GRAYNESS** is to take back the seed! Let's go!"

Face-to-Face
with Hordus

You've discovered my secret!" the wizard shrieked. "Now I can't let you leave. For you, there shall be no ESCAPE!"

As we ran toward the seed, Hordus flew across the room and blocked our path.

"What do you think you're doing, ridiculous beings? I'll use your hope and joy to **feed** the Infinite Seed!" he cried in a rage.

"You can't do this. The Infinite Seed doesn't belong to you, it is not yours!" said Lorian. "It belongs to the Kingdom of Blossom Valley, and now it's time for us to return it to its home."

"This IS its home!" the wizard boomed. "The Infinite Seed no longer exists. Now it is this magnificent creature, which I created to serve me! I call it the Seed of Destruction. Thanks to this, my

POWER is growing. Soon, my beauty will be so dazzling that it will obscure the light of the sun!"

"We will stop you and take back the seed!" the Wicked Witch shouted.

Hordus held up a hand. "Enough of this pointless chatter: I will destroy you!"

With that, he summoned a burst of **LIGHTNING**!

We ducked behind some golden statues that

were as bright as mirrors. The **lightning bolts** bounced from one statue to the next . . . and dissipated!

The wizard was about to fire off another spell when the seed moved, as if by magic. He hadn't commanded it!

But I knew what was happening — INVISIBLE Winglet was trying to take the seed!

"What is going on?" Hordus shouted, turning in circles.

As soon as Winglet had her hands on the flower bud, a bright light shone. She reappeared before our eyes!

"Winglet!" Lorian shouted.

But it was only for a moment.

The light vanished, the empress started to slowly turn invisible again, and the SEED turned into a horrible black clump.

"Oh no!" we all cried.

"How dare you!" the wizard shrieked.

Hordus was furious.

Winglet was fading, and Hordus summoned

all his strength to stand up and conjure one last burst of lightning. He was moving quickly, but my mousely instincts were stronger than my fear. I quickly threw myself in front of the empress and **shielded** her with my body!

I closed my eyes, preparing to become a mouse meatball . . . but Hordus's lightning bolt didn't strike me! It was shattered by a golden light and disappeared in a cascade of sparkles.

That dazzling light had been released from the seed. It was even more intense than the LIGHT that had erupted when Winglet had touched it!

The petals of the flower bud began to turn brighter, and the black color faded away like a distant nightmare. The flower bud turned a beautiful warm golden color. It filled us all with hope and joy. The seed wasn't evil anymore!

Winglet had reappeared, and this time she didn't disappear again. The seed was safe, and the sorcery that had transformed the empress into a Shapeless One had vanished.

Winglet's face was wet with tears, which fell onto the seed in her hands.

"**NOOOOO!**" shouted Hordus. His beautiful face transformed into a terrifying sneer. We all took a couple of steps away from him in shock. "This is a spell that I cannot defeat — the light of **pure friendship**!"

With a final shout, the wizard dissolved into a black cloud. It swirled until it vanished into nothing.

"I can't believe it!" I squeaked, my heart pounding with happiness. "We did it! The Infinite Seed has been saved! The empress is with us again!"

Winglet hugged us tightly, and happy tears fell from her eyes. "I can finally hug each and every one of you!" she said between sobs.

"I don't know about that!" the Wicked Witch said, putting her hands up. But it was too late, Winglet had already wrapped her arms around the witch.

"Sorry," Winglet said, quickly stepping back. But the witch surprised everyone by pulling Winglet in for a hug.

"Oh, why not!" she said.

Lorian smiled at her. "I think it was your

TEARS that saved the seed, Winglet, and the Knight's noble act. The light of friendship is so strong that it overcomes all evil!"

Even the gray paint that Merlin had covered us with had vanished, as if by magic.

I didn't know exactly what had happened, but I knew one thing: I was fabumousely happy to have Winglet back again!

THE RETURN OF THE KINGDOM OF BLOSSOM VALLEY

We left Hordus's palace, eager to complete our goal: to REPLANT the Infinite Seed on Hazy Mountain.

Now that we could see Winglet again and our mission was almost complete, I felt as though my heart had wings!

Once we got back to the summit of Hazy Mountain, we reunited with Dawn, Narek, and the crocodile. They had been vigilantly keeping **watch** at the entrance of the underground world.

Winglet greeted them affectionately, then turned to me and handed me the seed. "I would like you to replant it, Knight. It's thanks to you that the **EMPIRE** has been saved."

I blushed with embarrassment.

"This is too great an honor, Empress!"

"Maybe," Winglet said with a kind smile. "But you deserve it."

"Let's do it together," I said.

So, trembling, I took the flower bud in my paws. With Winglet's help, I deposited it in the soil where it had once grown.

As soon as its roots touched the soil, a light as intense as a star burst out of the seed. Holey cheese!

We all had to close our eyes. When we reopened them, as if by magic, the mud had been washed away, the stink disappeared, and the Great Grayness was replaced by great color. All of the Kingdom of Swamp Valley began to cloak itself in green! The boggy marshlands burst with shining water, tall trees stretched toward the sky, bright flowers dotted emerald-green fields, and the gray sky turned a delicate azure blue. The air was

suddenly filled with a sweet **SCENT**!
King Multicolor's Underground People slowly returned aboveground. The people of Swamp Valley, who had been so sad, began to **smile** now that the gray had been replaced with color.

After thousands of years, the **KINGDOM OF BLOSSOM VALLEY** had been freed from Hordus's sorcery and

Come!

The colors are back!

Hooray!

returned to its true splendor!

"At last, the empire will be able to live in the peace that we've awaited for so long," Winglet cried in joy.

"I've never seen such **beauty**!" I squeaked under my breath.

"Me neither!" a small voice cried.

The voice continued. "The Kingdom of Blossom Valley is even more beautiful than before. There

Hooray!

Now the Kingdom of Blossom Valley shines!

are so many colors for me to pose against!"

"Gray Chameleon!" we cried, thrilled to see him again.

"Just Chameleon now, please," he corrected us.

The gray was just a memory. Chameleon's scales already shone with so many **COLORS**!

"Chameleon will be in charge of classifying all the new colors," a regal voice boomed. King Multicolor had returned aboveground to admire the return of the Kingdom of Blossom Valley.

"I don't know how to thank you," he said with a bow. "Our *dream*, and the dream of our ancestors, has come true, thanks to your courage. You've restored our life. We will never forget you!"

"Thank you for your help," said Winglet. "And for believing in us, for not giving up. You have also shown great **courage**."

We bid farewell to our new friends, determined

to keep their marvemouse, colorful country in our hearts.

As usual, Lorian knew the right thing to say as we departed. "Joy appears even more splendid after having lost it."

He looked right at Winglet as he spoke. I'm sure that he wasn't just talking about the Kingdom of Blossom Valley!

Joy appears even more splendid after you've lost it!

RETURN TO THE LAND OF BOOKS

We returned to the River of Boredom, which had transformed into a lively, crystal-clear torrent of water, and boarded our ship. We were eager to return to the **LAND OF BOOKS** and see it freed it from the Great Grayness.

As soon as we reached the border, we ran into Alice, the three musketeers, Robin Hood, and the White Rabbit. They were all back to normal!

"Our world has been **SAVED**!" cried Alice as we disembarked.

The White Rabbit hopped around as usual. In the background, we could hear the Queen of Hearts shouting, "Off with their heads!"

"Even she's back to normal . . . unfortunately," Alice added, **hiding** from the Queen.

The musketeers were once again the fearless

swordsmen they'd always been, and the effects of the **GReaT GRaYNess** had disappeared! A small crowd of characters had already gathered around us.

"Captain Hook and the Wicked Witch of the West conquered the Great Grayness!" they cheered.

"Ha, ha, ha!" Hook snickered to the Wicked Witch. "What did I tell you? Fame and success guaranteed! Wait and see how they **ReACT** when they find out how we beat Hordus."

The characters ran up and raised them into the air. "For the witch and the captain! Hip, hip, hooray! Hip, hip, hooray!"

"Hmmm," said the witch. "It doesn't seem like we're **scaring** them one bit. In fact, they almost seem to like us!"

"Oh, thats all right. We'll regain our evilness another day," said Hook. "For now, let's enjoy the party!"

Even Peter Pan and Dorothy had come to greet us. The Wicked Witch of the West and Captain Hook were **eager** to get back to frightening them!

They're heroes!

Wahoo!

Hooray!

Long live the Land of Books!

Hooray!

"Remember the PROMISE you made to Euridice the mole," Winglet told them. "She could come aboveground and flatten you into paperweights!"

"Ha, ha, ha!" Hook cried. "Empress, I can see that your usual good humor has returned!"

The witch grinned wickedly. "Um, Hooky . . . I think your CROCODILE has also returned."

Captain Hook's number one enemy had already begun to eye his prey hungrily. After a long journey, he was ready for a snack!

"RAISE ANCHOR!" Hook shouted, climbing back onto his ship, followed by the crocodile. As we watched him set sail, I waved. The poor captain, on the run again!

"Ha, ha, ha!" the witch cackled. "I'll miss that old treasure hunter! Now, where's my little Dorothy? Ah, there she is . . ."

She was about to chase after Dorothy when the

ground trembled beneath our feet and Euridice's **SNOUT** popped out!

"My friends!" the mole cried. "After learning about this land full of fictional characters, I thought I'd move here! The Land of Books is the ideal home for a **BOOK LOVER** like me. Hey — what are you doing, Witch?"

"Oh, nothing, nothing!" the Wicked Witch of the West said, whistling.

What are you doing?

Winglet, Lorian, and I watched with glee as the witch tried to figure out how to *chase* Dorothy without the mole noticing.

In the end, it was important for Captain Hook and the Wicked Witch to save their nemeses from the Great Grayness.

After all, an evil character doesn't exist without a good character!

THE EMPIRE
HAS BEEN SAVED

We said farewell to our friends, promising to see them very, very soon. I would see them as soon as I flipped through the **books** in my library at home!

When we arrived at Crystal Castle, Blossom greeted us, glowing with happiness. Winglet ran and **hugged** her, holding her mother tight for a long time.

"Forgive me, Mother, if I was too impulsive," she said at last.

"Winglet, it's you who must forgive me," said Blossom. "You have learned so much. I wanted to protect you, but in the end, your choice was the better path. After reuniting the empire, you demonstrated that you know how to do the most difficult thing of all: protect and govern it."

My **heart** softened like melted mozzarella.

Blossom turned to me and Lorian. "Thank you, noble knights. As always, you were there for my Winglet every step of the way."

The empress smiled. "It's thanks to them that I'm here at all. You two are the greatest **friends** of the empire!"

"Oh, Winglet. You risked so much for us," I

said. I didn't want to say anything more specific. I was afraid of worrying Blossom!

"Speaking of which," I added, turning to Winglet and lowering my voice, "I'm curious about something: What's the **NiNtH** word from the Parchment of Positivity? You said it before you turned into a Shapeless One, right?"

Winglet gave me a wink. "It's the same word that saved the seed, the most beautiful and positive word of all: fRiendShip."

Cheese niblets, of course! "How did you figure that out?"

"I memorized and repeated the eight words that we had found by accident," Winglet said. "Then I thought about what was missing. And then it hit me! I figured out the ninth word — fRiendShip — was the only positive word that wouldn't turn me into a Shapeless One forever."

Winglet looked lost in thought. "So I said it,

even though I didn't know what would happen after that! I knew becoming shapeless was the best way to get out of that prison. But the light of friendship, which shone from your **noble** action, freed me from that terrible curse!"

She took my paws and gazed at me with her bright blue eyes. With the **crown** shining on her head, I knew deep in my fur that she was the most marvemouse empress the Empire of Fantasy could ever have: the REBEL EMPRESS!

A Trip Over the Kingdom of Blossom Valley

fter a great feast to celebrate our return, we were eager to admire a panoramic view of beautiful KINGDOM OF BLOSSOM VALLEY!

"You must see it with your own eyes, Mother," the empress said. "Otherwise you won't believe it!"

Winglet, Lorian, and I invited Blossom to join us in the hot-air balloon to observe the countryside from above. The wind ruffled my whiskers and fur, and even though I'm afraid of heights, I tried to enjoy myself. It was a truly fabumouse sight!

"Mother, that's the LAND OF BOOKS," Winglet said, pointing to the plains and valleys where the breeze rustled the pages.

"That must be Hook's ship," said Lorian with

a grin. "He's still trying to escape the crocodile!"

We all burst out laughing, waving in the direction of our friend.

At last, we spied the Kingdom of Blossom Valley. The intoxicating scent of **flowers** reached all the way to the sky!

"How incredible," Blossom said. "Nature is flourishing even more than the legends predicted!"

We enjoyed the view, admiring the flowering fields, the valleys, and the hills. It seemed impawssible that this marvemouse **splendor** was only mud and sadness days ago!

Suddenly, in the **distance**, we glimpsed a field that was a darker color.

"What's that over there?" Winglet asked.

"I have no idea," I said.

As we got closer, it became even darker . . . black . . . threatening . . . until a sight came into focus before our very eyes.

The sight froze my whiskers!

At the border of the Kingdom of Blossom Valley, an immense field full of Seeds of Destruction was growing!

"No! That's not possible," said Winglet.

"HA, HA, HA, HA, HA, HA!"

echoed through the valley. Hordus!

Even though our hot-air balloon was still flying far above, we understood the terrible truth. Hordus's plan was even bigger than we'd imagined . . .

"He wants to build another empire," Winglet said, eyes wide. "Every seed will give birth to an evil realm!"

HOW TOTALLY TERRIFYING!

For now, the Empire of Fantasy was safe — but an evil attack was coming!

The hot-air balloon continued to float, pushed by the wind, which seemed to get stronger and stronger . . .

Suddenly, the balloon started to *spin*, *spin*, *spin*, and my head also started to *spin*, *spin*, *spin*, until . . .

I FAINTED!

Look!

A New
Adventure!

When I woke up, I found myself at the flea market in New Mouse City, surrounded by junk.

Great globs of Gouda, what had happened?

Now I remembered! Before I was tossed into the Empire of Fantasy, I had been trying to get back my beloved **TOY TRAIN**!

Creepella was whispering in my ear. "Cheesepuff, I'm sorry that your little train was sold. I'd be more than happy to give you my favorite Toy from when I was a mouselet. Maybe that would help!"

She gave me a creepy doll made of different fabric sewn together. "Thank you, Creepella!" I said. "What a lovely bat — I mean duck . . ."

Creepella was offended. "Can't you see it's clearly a **mouse**?"

"Oh, of course!" I squeaked. I held on tight to Creepella's creature. Even though it had three ears, one eye, a horn on its face, and bat wings, it was the best toy I had ever been given, because it meant something to Creepella!

That evening, before I went to sleep, I thought about the thousands of adventures that my beloved toy train would have with other mouselets. Sometimes all it takes is a little imagination

For you!

and a crew of unforgettable heroes — including a captain with a hook for a hand and a witch who wasn't all that evil.

Their ADVENTURES are recorded here, in the book you're reading! I hope that you've enjoyed them, because the best stories are the ones that continue to live within us for a long, long time.

Or my name isn't

Geronimo Stilton!

GAME
SOLUTIONS

Robin Hood is located in the upper right, in the woods

The map of the Kingdom of Swamp Valley is on the

second shelf to the right of the window.

Here are all the places where Gray Chameleon is hiding.

This is the path to reach the exit.

Parchment of Positivity

Anyone who says one of these words in the Kingdom of Swamp Valley will instantly be turned into a Shapeless One!

1) Wonderful

2) Cheerful

3) Humor

4) Enchanting

5) Heart

6) Harmony

7) Imagination

8) Sweetness

9) Friendship

DON'T MISS HOW THE THEA SISTERS' FABUMOUSE TREASURE HUNT BEGAN!

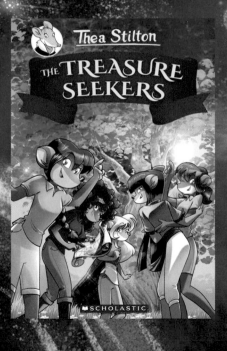

A SCOTTISH DREAM COME TRUE

Colette placed the last clip in her fur and **smiled** in satisfaction.

"There!" she squeaked. "I'm ready!"

She went to join the Thea Sisters in the room they had been sharing for a few weeks. But instead of finding her four best friends, she found only one.

"Where are the others?" *Colette* asked Violet, who was happily stuffing a backpack with a blanket, a travel pillow, and a camera.

I'm ready!

"Nicky is **feeding** the horses before we go," Violet explained. "Pam is in the kitchen making sandwiches, and Paulina —"

Before Violet could finish her sentence, the door flew open and Paulina entered, a **MAP** in her paws.

"For our picnic, Miss Kerr suggested we take the trail into the woods a few miles from here," she announced, excitedly pointing to a spot on the **MAP**. "She says there's a peaceful clearing with a *lovely* stream running through it."

"That sounds so beautiful!" Colette said, sighing wistfully. She **LOOKED** out the window at the bright emerald-green grass and the sheep, cows, and ponies that Nicky was feeding for the last time. "Oh, I'm so sad to be leaving Scotland already. **This vacation went by too quickly!**"

"You're right, Coco," Paulina agreed, "but it's not over yet!"

"Exactly," Violet added. "Let's enjoy the days we have left."

The friends **smiled** as they reflected on the wonderful vacation. It wasn't very long ago that Colette, Paulina, Violet, Nicky, and Pamela were at Mouseford Academy thinking about how they would **spend** their summer, when Paulina found an ad that seemed **perfect** for them.

> ### Do you want a different kind of vacation?
> # Scotland is waiting!
> Stay at an organic farm for free! In exchange, you'll help us take care of the garden and animals.

The Thea Sisters were excited by the idea

of visiting a beautiful farm where they would learn to take care of sheep and horses.

They immediately got in touch with Miss Kerr, the owner of the farm. Then they booked their flight from Whale Island and, in a short time, found themselves driving through the green countryside on their

SCOTLAND

Scotland is one of the four regions that make up the United Kingdom, along with Wales, England, and Northern Ireland. It covers the northern third of the island of Great Britain, and its landscape is rich with striking mountains, blue lakes, thick forests, and golden beaches. The famous Scottish Highlands region is known for its wild nature and beautiful castles.

SCOTLAND

Yum . . . shortbread!

Seals on the Scottish coast.

way to Miss Kerr's farm. That's how their very special summer started!

When the Thea Sisters arrived at the farm, Miss Kerr greeted them warmly and made them feel right at home with some of her delicious shortbreads — Scottish butter cookies — and *cranachan*, a *traditional* dessert made with raspberries, oats, honey, and cream.

Taking care of the garden and the animals was, of course, work, but it was also fun. Nicky in particular had really **taken to** two of the ponies on the farm. Plus, the five friends had rented an SUV and visited the surrounding areas, where they explored breathtaking **WATERFALLS**, **CAVES**, bays, and castles.

A charming Scottish castle.

The vacation had gone by in a flash, and they were almost at the end. Miss Kerr had suggested that the mouselets rest and **visit** all the things they hadn't seen before they had to leave. So that day the Thea Sisters had organized a **relaxing** picnic, and now they couldn't wait for their adventure.

"We have enough sandwiches for a week!" Pam exclaimed as she returned from the kitchen holding a basket of food, napkins, and utensils.

"And I've loaded the backpacks with everything we need," Violet said.

"Great!" Colette exclaimed. "Now let's get Nicky and go!"

This will be the best picnic!

A SUDDEN STORM

Half an hour later, Pam parked the SUV in a small parking lot at the edge of the woods.

"**Here we are!**" Paulina exclaimed happily. "The place Miss Kerr suggested is about a ten-minute **HIKE** down this trail."

Pam looked at the trailhead, confused. "It looks like **THREE** different paths begin here," she pointed out. "Did Miss Kerr mention which **trail** to take?"

Paulina scratched her head. "I don't know," she said, perplexed. "On the map, there's only **one**. Maybe they all lead to the same place."

"Maybe, or maybe not," Colette said wisely. "We'd better check!"

At that moment, a hiker approached and Colette flagged the mouse down.

"Excuse me," Colette asked, politely pointing to the map. "But could you tell me what path we should take to get **HERE**?"

The hiker barely glanced at the map. Instead she just looked up at the sky and shook her head. "**It's not worth it,**" she said.

Huh?

I warned you!

Colette was surprised. According to Miss Kerr, the spot sounded like the **perfect** place.

"But why not?" Colette replied. "We heard it was a nice spot for a picnic."

"Suit yourself," the rodent replied brusquely. "Take the first path on the left."

Colette went back to her friends to tell them the mouse's **answer**.

"How strange," Violet said.

"Maybe she just meant that there are **better** places around here," Nicky said with a shrug.

"There's only one way to find out," Pamela said **confidently**, and the five friends started down the trail. A short while later, they emerged from the woods in a beautiful clearing with a *spectacular* view of the mountains.

"Well, this place seems absolutely **perfect** to me!" Colette exclaimed happily. "There are so many flowers! And look at this *sparkling*, clear stream. I don't know what that mouse was talking about!"

"Yes, but be careful not to fall in," Pam warned. "The water will be **cold**."

Paulina laid the blankets on the grass and the **FIVE FRIENDS** could finally relax and enjoy the **marvemouse** view.

"Come on, let's take a photo!" Colette proposed as she finished the last bite of a piece of the cake that Miss Kerr had packed them.

"Oh, I think we've taken enough photos on this trip," Violet said as she lay back on the blanket and closed her eyes. "Right now, I just want to **relax**."

But a moment later, Violet sat straight up on the blanket.

"Hey!" she squeaked. "Who splashed me with water?"

Nicky looked worriedly at the sky, which had suddenly gone **DARK**.

You've never seen
Geronimo Stilton like this before!

Get your paws on the all-new

Geronimo Stilton

graphic novels. You've gouda* have them!

*Gouda is
a type
of cheese.

Don't miss a single fabumouse adventure!

Up Next:

Visit Geronimo in every univers

Spacemice

Geronimo Stiltonix and his crew are out of this world!

Cavemice

Geronimo Stiltonoot, an ancient ancestor, is friends with the dinosaurs in the Stone Age!

Miceking

Geronimo Stilton amongst the dra the ancient far

Catch up on these special adventures!

The Hunt for the Golden Book

The Hunt for the Curious Cheese

The Hunt for the Secret Papyrus

The Hunt for the Hundredth Key

The Hunt for the Colosseum Ghost

THE JOURNEYS THROUGH TIME

THE JOURNEY THROUGH TIME

2. BACK IN TIME

3. THE RACE AGAINST TIME

4. LOST IN TIME

5. NO TIME TO LOSE

6. THE TEST OF TIME

7. TIME WARP

Don't miss any of my adventures in the Kingdom of Fantasy!

THE KINGDOM OF FANTASY

THE QUEST FOR PARADISE:
THE RETURN TO THE KINGDOM OF FANTASY

THE AMAZING VOYAGE:
THE THIRD ADVENTURE IN THE KINGDOM OF FANTASY

THE DRAGON PROPHECY:
THE FOURTH ADVENTURE IN THE KINGDOM OF FANTASY

THE VOLCANO OF FIRE:
THE FIFTH ADVENTURE IN THE KINGDOM OF FANTASY

THE SEARCH FOR TREASURE:
THE SIXTH ADVENTURE IN THE KINGDOM OF FANTASY

THE ENCHANTED CHARM:
THE SEVENTH ADVENTURE IN THE KINGDOM OF FANTASY

THE PHOENIX OF DESTINY:
AN EPIC KINGDOM OF FANTASY ADVENTURE

THE HOUR OF MAGIC:
THE EIGHTH ADVENTURE IN THE KINGDOM OF FANTASY

THE WIZARD'S WAND:
THE NINTH ADVENTURE IN THE KINGDOM OF FANTASY

THE SHIP OF SECRETS:
THE TENTH ADVENTURE IN THE KINGDOM OF FANTASY

THE DRAGON OF FORTUNE:
AN EPIC KINGDOM OF FANTASY ADVENTURE

THE GUARDIAN OF THE REALM:
THE ELEVENTH ADVENTURE IN THE KINGDOM OF FANTASY

THE ISLAND OF DRAGONS:
THE TWELFTH ADVENTURE IN THE KINGDOM OF FANTASY

THE BATTLE FOR THE CRYSTAL CASTLE:
THE THIRTEENTH ADVENTURE IN THE KINGDOM OF FANTASY

THE KEEPERS OF THE EMPIRE:
THE FOURTEENTH ADVENTURE IN THE KINGDOM OF FANTASY

Thea Stilton

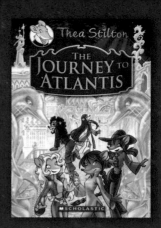

Secret Fairies

Don't miss any of these exciting series featuring the Thea Sisters!

Treasure Seekers

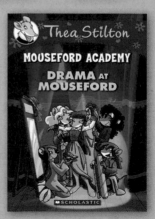

Mouseford Academy

Don't miss any of my fabumouse special editions!

THE JOURNEY TO ATLANTIS

THE SECRET OF THE FAIRIES

THE SECRET OF THE SNOW

THE CLOUD CASTLE

THE TREASURE OF THE SEA

THE LAND OF FLOWERS

THE SECRET OF THE CRYSTAL FAIRIES

THE DANCE OF THE STAR FAIRIES

THE MAGIC OF THE MIRROR